4
SUBWAY

VIOLET HUNTER

Matador
9 Priory Business Park,
Wistow Road, Kibworth Beauchamp,
Leicestershire. LE8 0RX
Tel: 0116 279 2299
Email: books@troubador.co.uk
Web: www.troubador.co.uk/matador
Twitter: @matadorbooks

ISBN 978 1785892 318

British Library Cataloguing in Publication Data.
A catalogue record for this book is available from the British Library.

Printed and bound by CPI Group (UK) Ltd, Croydon, CR0 4YY
Typeset in 11.5pt Garamond by Troubador Publishing Ltd, Leicester, UK

Matador is an imprint of Troubador Publishing Ltd

MIX
Paper from
responsible sources
FSC
www.fsc.org
FSC® C013604

To my sister Lucy

1

JIMMY

I turned the corner and a blast of freezing cold air slammed into my body. The estate's three tower blocks looked as if they were leaning in, like people talking. A metal grill covering the car park made a loud humming sound and rancid air rose up from the bins. Some old geezers were standing around outside the betting shop, trying to pretend it wasn't freezing cold. This country was crap.

Pushing open the door to the newsagents the headline, 'Migrants Blamed for Surge in Crime', jumped out at me. Yeah, that was true and they were stealing all the jobs.

Ahmed said, "Alright Jimmy?" handing me my usual packet of fags.

I grunted, "Not bad."

Ahmed was OK, the only one who was. Mum had fainted in his shop once and he brought her home.

I walked through the playground, with its scabby swings and roundabout, green paint peeling, rusty metal underneath. The path by the tracks was brightly lit then it got darker. A streetlamp was broken, no one bothered about fixing it. I got to the pub and went straight to the bar. Behind me I heard a loud croaking laugh. I bought a pint and went over.

"Alright mate," Chris said.

"Yeah."

Gary was slurping lager. He stuck his thumb up in greeting.

Dean just nodded.

"We heard Wayne's back," Chris said.

"You're joking." I put my pint down hard, spilling some on the floor.

He shook his head. "Nope. Nige told me. You heard him, Gary, didn't you?"

Gary nodded. "Said he saw him in the pub on Springer Street, looking like he'd never been away."

"Fuck."

"If things kick off we'll be here," Chris said.

"Thanks mate, I appreciate it."

I hadn't seen Wayne for a long time. I'd almost forgotten about him. Fucking bastard. For two years it's been like he's dead then he turns up again. My stomach started tensing up with dread, familiar, the same feeling I had all the time he was around.

I went to the bog for a piss, breathing in hard, trying to get rid of the tension.

When I got back Gary was reminiscing.

"Remember that beggar we done, Chris? You missed out there Jimmy. How come you're never around when there's any real action? Anyway I bet he's not swaggering around like he used to. Crawling more like." Gary had a big head and bulging eyes. "Oh no, don't hurt me please," he mimicked, looking at us, begging, like a dog. They rolled about laughing and I half joined in, pissed off with Gary for making out I was too scared to fight.

The fruit machine winked and flashed. There were two old girls sitting in a corner; apart from that no one else was there. It was the last pub left open near the estate.

"Watford on Saturday then," Chris said.

"6/0, I reckon," Gary said.

"We might let them get one past us in the first half, just so they think they've got a chance, losers," I said.

"Reckon we'll be going up soon," Chris said.

We got more drinks and the talk got cruder. Chris was telling us about two girls who he was seeing.

"I'm not that interested in either to be honest but they've both got big tits so I can't complain."

Finally the barman said, "Time you were going, boys."

On the way home I took a short cut through the alley. There was someone playing an accordion, a white cup in front of him. High notes were sounding through the passageway. He was getting into it, playing some foreign tune, like he was sad and homesick. Why didn't he go back then? I thought about what Gary said. He meant it as a kind of challenge. I'd had fights for sure, maybe not as many as Gary but it wasn't like I was trying to avoid them. Alcohol burned in my stomach and I thought with hatred about Wayne. I'd show them all.

I walked towards the beggar, my head down as if I was going to go past. His fingers were flying over the buttons. As I got close I aimed a kick at his body and he fell forwards. The accordion made a loud sigh as it crashed to the ground.

"No, please," he called out, trying to grab the instrument.

A feeling of power surged through my body and I kicked him again in the stomach. He groaned and made a weird gurgling sound, curling up trying to protect himself. Blood oozed from his nose.

Someone shouted, "Oi, stop that!"

There was a figure at the entrance to the alley. I ran, crossing the road, dodging a car, then raced into the park. I reached the far gate and headed for the car park behind the flats. I leant against a garage door, breathing hard to stop myself throwing up. Fuck, that felt good, scary but good. I waited until I'd got my breath back then started walking, darting looks behind to see if anyone was following, listening out for sirens but for once it was quiet. The adrenaline stopped pumping and the sweat on my back was going cold.

When I got in Liam was on the sofa watching TV.

"Alright? What you watching?"

"Good film. Where've you been?" He glanced my way.

"Just down the pub." I thought he might notice something but his eyes went straight back to the screen. It was OK anyway – he'd never grass on me. Me and him got on.

Mum came out of the kitchen and said, "Have you eaten, Jimmy?" She sounded tired.

"I'll make some toast."

Later in the bathroom I looked in the mirror. My face was whiter than usual. I studied my hands – nothing on them – looked at my clothes – no blood. I wondered what I'd have done if the person hadn't shouted at me to stop. I was angry and ready to really go at him. What did that mean? I still had the sick feeling in my stomach but there was something else as well – a sense of satisfaction, because for once I had power over someone else.

* * *

Next day Chris and me were in the cafe on the high street. It was just us, plus some old guy, chewing chips with his two teeth. The area was shit now, foreign food shops spreading out onto the pavement, polluting our streets.

I told him about the beggar.

"Good job mate," he nodded. "While we're on the subject, I've got a proposal."

"Oh yeah?"

"We agree that Pakis, niggers and immigrants should be sent back, right?"

"Yeah, they're taking over this country."

Mum hadn't had a holiday for years. The shop she worked in made her go part-time because foreigners wanted her job, so now she had to do office cleaning as well.

When I was at school there was loads of shit about people being equal; some of the teachers went over the top about how black people had a hard time but I didn't see it that way. Seemed to me they got all the privileges. There was a gang of them at my school. They were arrogant, went around intimidating us. Some of the white kids sucked up to them, tried talking the same and doing the swagger but I kept out of their way. Once they'd cornered me. Two of them stood with their feet on my arms, pressing down hard so the blood drained out of my fingers. The other one pulled a knife out of his pocket. He said he didn't like the way I looked at him and I needed to watch it or I'd be dead meat.

"It's time to take action, we can't just sit around on our arses doing nothing. The New English Right wants more people; I'm joining, you up for it?" Chris said.

I remembered Dad telling me stories about being in the

National Front. The demonstrations they used to go on were massive. Black people were really scared. It sounded like a good time.

"Count me in."

Chris gave me a playful punch on the shoulder.

"Great. Next meeting's Thursday, 7.30 p.m., the Swan in Denham Street."

2

VALERIE

If anyone asked what my job was I told them I was an actor but right then I was behind a counter, coffee machine on my right, a row of cakes on my left. It was my fourth shift that week. If it went on like this I'd have to give up on my dream of becoming a great Shakespearean actor. My plan had been to start with characters like Rosalind, Juliet and Miranda, then move on to playing Gertrude and Cleopatra. So many great roles. I loved the hugeness of his plays, the wars, the death and the madness. One day I wanted to play Lady Macbeth.

It was quiet in the cafe. Like a tide everyone had flowed back to the office. Teresa was out the back having a break. I was thinking about the audition next week, my fourteenth since leaving college. Sometimes if I was nervous I spoke too fast or fluffed a line but other times I knew I'd got it right and still the answer was no. It was getting difficult to keep faith in myself.

This play, *Wounded Home*, was about the effects of war, not just on the men but on the rest of the family, particularly the women. The main character was Paul, a soldier returning from Afghanistan. I was trying for the role of his girlfriend,

Chrissie, who was twenty-four, exactly my age. I really wanted the part.

I was wiping down the coffee machine with my back to the counter when someone said, "Skinny cappuccino please."

Turning I saw Anton, a big smile on his face. He was wearing a dark blue jacket and an orange shirt. Compared to the drab brown furniture in the cafe he looked amazing.

"Hey! Great to see you."

"Thought I'd check out how you're doing. I was going to phone to say I was coming then thought I'd surprise you instead."

"It's been ages, what've you been up to?"

"Seeing my aunt and uncle in the States. I got back a couple of weeks ago. How are you doing?"

I shrugged and looked around at the crowded tables and chairs, the plates with crumbs on, the photos of snow-covered mountains on the wall. "This is my stage now."

He looked sympathetic. "You'll get something soon, you're too good not to. It's only been a few months. Talking of stages – I've got a spare ticket for *Twelfth Night* on Friday. Leila can't make it and I thought of you. It should be good."

"Thanks so much. I meant to get a ticket but I left it too late and it'd sold out."

"Have you had any auditions recently?"

I told him about my failures and about the part I was preparing for.

"The play sounds great – I can imagine you as Chrissie."

"Hope they can too. I'll go mad if I work here much longer."

"I've got some news," he said, leaning across the counter.

"Tell me."

"I've been offered a part in a musical."

"Fantastic," I said, genuinely pleased. Anton's passion was musical theatre whereas I really struggled with singing. "What's it about?"

"A group of prison inmates form a band inside then try to carry on playing when they get out. The company's based in Sheffield. I'll be moving up there temporarily."

I felt a pang. "That's a long way to go."

"It's only a short run. I'll be back again soon."

My hand was on the counter between us and he rested his briefly on mine. It felt light as a feather.

"See you Friday then," he said, waving as he went out the door.

When he'd gone I realised I'd been missing him. We'd been close at drama school but now work or other things got in the way and we saw each other less often.

Teresa came in from the back room.

"Everything OK? Who was that you were talking to?"

"My friend Anton, from college."

We were only friends but when he was talking I felt something more and wondered whether it was coming from him or me. There was something about the way he'd looked at me when he left. I shook off the feeling. I was probably imagining it. He was going out with Leila and I'd decided never to get involved with a man who was with someone. It wasn't really a moral thing just that life was complicated enough without that.

* * *

Anton's success inspired me and I used every spare minute I had to rehearse. By the time the audition came I was ready. I could have spoken the lines hanging upside down if they asked me to.

At the theatre I found the toilets, checking that I looked OK. I was wearing eyeliner but no other make-up, my hair was shoulder length and I'd had it straightened. I was turning from the mirror to leave when a young woman came through the doors. She was panting a little.

"Do you know where the auditions are?" she asked.

"I'll show you if you like."

"Thanks, if you're not too busy."

It took a moment to realise what she meant, then I noticed a broom leaning against the wall near me and felt a jab of pain.

I said straight away, "I'm here for the auditions too."

"Oh sorry, I didn't realise. It's just that…"

Her pale skin went pink and she turned away, unable to look me in the eye. Fumbling with the door handle she went out. I stood still, feeling humiliated, tears coming into my eyes. She really thought I was there to clean the toilet. I went into a cubicle, sat on the seat and wept quietly. It was like she'd told me to stay in my place, that I mustn't step out of it, I couldn't be somebody different or special. Acting was for those like her, not black girls like me.

I thought about my dad. He'd have put his arm around me and said, "Go ahead and cry. Cry as hard as you like, then go out and do as you intended to do."

I blew my nose and went to the mirror to check my eyeliner. It had run so I wiped it away and reapplied it then I drew myself up and went out of the door.

Auditions were being held for several parts and nearly every seat in the green room was taken. I sat in the opposite corner to the girl, avoiding her eye. A name was called and she got up. As she went out the door I wondered if she was auditioning for the same role as me.

Two more people were called then it was my turn. I stood in the wings and took a deep breath then walked onto the stage. Three people were sitting in the front row, a man and two women. I told them my name and the piece I was going to perform and one of the women said, "Please begin."

The monologue I'd chosen was by Irina, from Chekhov's *Three Sisters*. Pausing for a moment I let the character wash over me. The words came easily. My body stayed loose as I moved around the stage. I was still upset by the incident in the toilet but I used some of the emotion I felt and put it into my performance. I could tell it was good.

At the end of the speech I gave a bow. They thanked me and smiled but gave nothing away. When I left the theatre the blonde girl was nowhere to be seen.

3

JIMMY

Liam wanted me to go fishing with him. I hadn't been for months so I said yes.

We left the house as it was getting light and got the bus to Clear Water. The place was deserted and we found a good spot with two wooden platforms. Liam had dyed the maggots with turmeric and inside the bait box were hundreds of gold wriggling creatures. I screwed the sections of my rod together and began threading line through the rings. I was out of practice and Liam was ready first. He stood at the side of the lake, paused for a moment, then with a quick flick cast out the line. It whipped through the air, landing close to the centre of the lake. He turned and grinned at me, as if to say *beat that*. I moved to the edge and did the same but it was a crap attempt and I only just missed an overhanging branch.

We sat on boxes close together, watching. It was quiet there, away from the noise of London. A slight breeze was blowing on the surface of the water making ripples. A cold mist hung above the lake and I zipped my jacket up. Though I didn't want to I thought about Wayne.

He was on my case from the day I was born. You

never knew where you were with him. Sometimes he was OK and other times he was mad. He would lure you in, be very friendly and then turn on you. The last time we fought wasn't the worst but it was the one I remembered. It was a few years back. I'd borrowed his games console and was playing on it when it broke. At first he pretended it was no big deal, he'd wait until I could pay him back, then one night he came back drunk and told me I had to get him a new one the next day – if I didn't have the money I'd have to steal one. When I said I couldn't he started pushing me around. I fought back and he punched me in the stomach. I fell over, twisting my wrist. I was screaming with the pain which was worse than anything I'd ever felt. Wayne just walked out of the house. Soon after that he left. I didn't know exactly what happened, but I thought Mum must have told him to go.

As if he knew what I was thinking Liam said, "He won't be around for long. You know what he's like, he'll hook up with another girl soon, though God knows what anyone sees in him."

I hated the fact that I was still intimidated by Wayne and that Liam knew it.

"Things are changing," I said.

"Oh yeah?"

I hadn't told him I was thinking of joining the NER. He was different to me about ethnics; he had a Paki friend, Nitin. Stupid name. He mentioned him quite often like he was something special. If I thought about it longer I could get suspicious because Liam didn't have any girlfriends. He never brought Nitin to the house though; he must have known he wouldn't be welcomed with open arms.

"He'll find out if I bump into him again."

He looked a bit doubtful but nodded.

We didn't talk much after that in case we disturbed the fish. The mist crept round behind and I could feel cold drops on the back of my neck. I pulled the hood of my fleece over my head, sank my neck into the warm fabric and breathed out.

There was a tug on my line.

Liam said, "Looks like a big one, don't let it go."

His tail was thrashing hard on the water. I gave extra line then reeled him in. Up he came. He was big, at least 15 pounds; a carp. We were having a battle; he leapt in the air and twisted round, eyes wide, flopped down and then up again but each time it wasn't as high. At last we got him into the net and on the landing mat. Liam got his phone out, I held the fish up and he took a photo. Then I put him back in the water and he swam away.

We stayed a while longer but there was no more action and Liam said, "I'm starving, let's go and get a burger."

"I'll come with you next weekend if you want," I said.

He laughed. "Think you'll catch another? You just got lucky that time."

"You're jealous. Never mind, your older brother will teach you how to do it."

As we walked back across the park he said, "You've been seeing Shelley a lot, you'll be getting married soon."

"Don't be stupid."

"I can hear wedding bells, you'll be down that aisle, kids, mortgage, all that stuff," he said.

"Yeah, yeah, in your dreams."

* * *

Shelley was working behind the bar at the White Horse when I first met her. Later she got a job in a wine bar. She had long black hair and was very pretty. I watched as she poured the drinks. Even though she was small she could handle the punters.

It was her eighteenth in two weeks and I wanted to get her something special. At her favourite clothes shop nothing caught my eye so I tried the one next door. Looking through the rails I spotted a silver top made from a sort of metallic material that was flexible. It would look really good with her black hair. I picked up the price tag. It was a lot. I left the shop feeling bad that I couldn't afford it. It was shit working and not having much left over after paying for travelling and fags. I'd been working for Uncle Ray for a few months. I liked him, he didn't promise things and then go back on them like Dad used to but he didn't pay a lot.

When I was young I wanted to design cars. I drew shape after shape, more and more fancy, state of the art, filling notebooks. I had separate pages for seats, dashboard and wheel hubs. I wanted to turn up at some really gorgeous girl's house in the car I designed, say, 'Yeah, this one's my latest model.'

I was going to do an engineering course but the teachers said it was no good just being good at drawing; you had to know about maths, 3D volumes, model scales. I was useless with numbers. After they said that I gave up thinking about it. I hated seeing new cars come out; they were crap and I knew I could have done better. After school I started a plumbing course but failed the first year. I tried getting other work but there was nothing going.

One day Ray came round and said, "I'll give you a try out

with the decorating business, Jimmy. I need to do something to help your mum, she doesn't look too good."

I hadn't done much painting before but I said yes. I didn't have much choice. Ray said if I worked hard he might take me on permanently. I'd been doing it for a few months now. I didn't really like the work but I did it as well as I could, took my time, clearing up drips, keeping my hand steady with the brush.

Ray liked Shelley and said he'd give me an extra thirty quid towards her present so I bought the silver top, wrapping it in red paper to make it look really special. We were going for an Italian but I went round her house first because I wanted her to wear the top out. I watched as she unwrapped it. She gasped as she took it out.

"It's lovely Jimmy," she said, holding it up and admiring herself in the mirror. "It must have cost a fortune."

I shrugged and smiled. "Whatever it was you're worth it."

She put it on. It looked even better than I imagined. She kissed me full on the mouth. I pulled her closer. The top was like snakeskin covering her body.

Later at the restaurant I ordered some sparkling wine and we toasted her being eighteen.

She said, "This is it. I'm going to make a new start now. I'm giving up working in the wine bar soon. I thought the tips would be good but I'm still not making enough to save anything. I might go to college to do a course, events management maybe."

I didn't like the idea of her studying; she might meet other blokes who fancied her.

"Isn't that just organising things?" I said.

"It'd make a change from people ordering you about, you should hear the things people say to me sometimes. The posher they are the worse they treat me."

I didn't want to argue on her birthday so I said she should do it if it was going to make her happy.

"Maybe after I've done the course we could get a place together. That'd be nice, wouldn't it?" she said, leaning across the table and kissing me.

"So long as we can do what we did earlier every night," I said.

We left the restaurant and got the Tube. We were walking back to hers when I saw Chris and Dean coming towards us. I cursed under my breath. Shelley couldn't stand Chris.

"Well, well, it's that loved-up twosome," Chris said.

He looked pissed. Dean was swaying from side to side.

"Alright," I said, hoping we could get away quick but Chris wasn't having any of it.

"You look gorgeous Miss Shelley, good enough to eat. Sorry, didn't mean it like that."

Shelley blushed.

"Fuck off Chris, we're having a special night, we don't need your crap," I said.

Dean was leering and I wanted to punch him. Chris wouldn't shut up. I could sense Shelley tensing up beside me.

I said, "Come on Shelley, let's go," but she pulled away from me, went up to Chris and said, "You know what, you're really stupid. You're trying to come on to me so you can divide me and Jimmy. It won't work, so forget it."

Then she turned away and started walking up the road. Chris had a look of mock fear on his face and Dean was laughing.

Chris said, "She's got you right where she wants you Jimmy, no mistake."

"Yeah well, it's her birthday, she can do what she likes; you two better piss off or…"

"Oh yeah, what have you got in mind?" Chris moved closer.

I didn't want any trouble so I laughed and clapped him on the shoulder. "Only joking. See you later."

I caught up with Shelley. "They're just pissed; they didn't mean anything by it."

"They're morons. Did you see the way Dean looked at me?"

"I'll keep away from him if it makes you happy."

"And Chris?"

She caught my expression and turned away.

4

VALERIE

I was round at Renee's, eating the vegetable lasagne she'd made, which was delicious.

"I haven't heard about the audition which probably means I didn't get it. I'm so fed up."

"You'll be fine. Something good's around the corner, just you wait and see," she said, waving a fork laden with pasta at me.

"OK, wise woman, I'm trying to believe you," I said, laughing.

Renee had been on the drama course with Anton and me. I thought she was a good actor but she suffered from really bad pre-performance nerves. She'd tried all sorts of relaxation and breathing exercises but nothing seemed to work. After graduation she decided to become a teacher instead. She seemed happy.

Turned out she was right about the audition because the next day I got an email calling me back. I was excited and was immediately dreaming about beginning professional rehearsals, then I had to remind myself that I was only halfway there and the really hard part was yet to come.

I'd been given two scenes to learn and started straight away, working on them every spare minute. One was a monologue by Chrissie, in which she was trying to cope with her boyfriend's moods. To begin with it was hard to find her voice and understand her character. I couldn't imagine being in her situation, having a partner whose job was fighting a war, not knowing when they left for work if you'd ever see them again. I read the lines over and over and gradually she began to take shape in my mind. I put the script down and began to walk around the room. I used my whole body when I was searching for a character, speaking the words standing up, lying down, walking around the room. Slowly I started to feel my way into her skin.

In the second scene Chrissie had an argument with Paul. The actor playing him had already been cast and we'd be doing the scene together. I asked Renee round to stand in for him.

"I don't mind helping you, as long as I'm nowhere near a stage," she said. We went over and over the scene, only stopping to stretch and drink water. I'd been given this chance and I was determined to really go for it.

At the audition I met the actor playing Paul, whose name was Richard, for the first time. He was white and didn't look anything like I'd imagined but from the moment we began the scene it was clear that the timing worked and our argument sounded real enough. After he'd exited the stage I took my place, ready for the monologue.

I'd practised the transition between scenes, slowing my speech and movement right down, addressing the imaginary audience on one side of the auditorium and then the other. At the end I bowed and left the stage, pleased with how it went but no idea what the outcome would be.

On the bus next day I got an email. I'd been offered the part of Chrissie. I studied my phone. Looked away then back again. The words were still there. First rehearsal on Wednesday, come prepared to work. A smile formed and, at the same time, tears. I looked out the window. As the bus crossed Waterloo Bridge, the sun was low in the west, clouds spreading out like fingers.

* * *

Rehearsals started. The director, Lucy, had a huge reputation so when I met her I was surprised how small and quietly spoken she was. She had a clear vision of what she wanted, rarely praised us but I liked her; I could tell that everything she asked us to do was because she wanted the play to work better.

Becoming closer to the character of Chrissie I began to think more about the history of war and wondered how many women had been in her situation. Their husbands or sons coming home from war after months, sometimes years away, often looking just the same until gradually the scars started to reveal themselves.

I worked hard. My clothes were often soaked with sweat. I was in many of the scenes and there were few places where I could drop my level of concentration. Some of the action was physical – at one rehearsal Richard caught my arm harder than usual and my cry of pain was real.

"I'm really sorry Valerie, I misjudged it, it won't happen again," he said.

Apart from doing some weekend shifts at the cafe I had little time for anything else. I didn't mind though, it was the life I wanted.

One night I was lying on the sofa, recovering from a particularly long rehearsal when Anton called.

"How're the rehearsals going?"

"Hard work, but I love it."

"Good, that's how it should be."

"What about the musical?" I said.

"Great, it's sold out every night. They're extending the run."

"That's amazing."

"Trouble is Leila's annoyed. She was here last weekend; we had a row. She said she didn't like me being away so much. I said it might be like this until I get established and she said it's not how she wants to live. I don't know if it's going to work out."

He'd been going out with Leila for about a year. I'd met her once. She was a beautiful Asian woman, training to be a lawyer.

"That's sad," I said. I couldn't tell from his tone what he was feeling.

"She wants life planned and organised. I said that's difficult when you're an actor, you have to take what comes."

"Perhaps it's hard for people with normal jobs to understand."

"Maybe you're right. Anyway, I wondered if you wanted to come up to see the show before you open? You could stay over." There was a slight pause. "I'll sleep on the sofa."

We laughed a little.

"Definitely," I said.

After the phone call I sat looking out of the window. The plane trees had lost their leaves, exposing the long, elegant branches. A young couple was walking through the park; they looked as if they were newly in love or lust and couldn't wait to be together in private. I thought about Anton. Strong feelings were trying to surface but I pushed them down. I had other things to focus on.

5

JIMMY

It was cold and I was walking fast, taking the short cut by the tracks. The arches made dark shadows across the path. Old drinks cans were stuck in between the struts and on the spikes of the grey metal fence: Carlsberg Special, Diamond Ice.

Up ahead someone stepped out from behind a wall. Two others appeared alongside. Fear leapt into my throat like bile. One was Asian, the other two black. I could smell skunk. I looked behind me but the road was a long way back. There was nothing else to do but go on. I was level – they stepped back like they were going to let me go past – then one jumped forward and grabbed me. He shoved his face into mine.

"Give us your phone."

The other two were going through my pockets. I was nearly pissing myself. Any moment there'd be a knife in my side. I pulled the phone out. I couldn't speak.

He grabbed it and laughed. "Good decision, white boy."

They moved back into the dark spaces and I ran. I reached the safety of the estate and looked back. They were nowhere to be seen. It was almost like it had never happened except that I was shaking and my phone was gone.

* * *

That night I decided. The bastards weren't going to get away with it – I was joining the NER.

Thursday night. The room was crammed to overflowing. Most looked ordinary, not like members of a right-wing army. There were quite a few women too, even one really attractive one who was sitting near me. People were calling across the room.

"Oi, Stevie, see you got a new haircut, who are you trying to impress? Your missus left you has she?"

"Shut it mate, just cos yours did a runner with a Paki." Laughter and jeers followed.

The last person sat down and the doors were locked. Tyler, the leader, stood up and the room went quiet. He was handsome: dark hair, a smart suit. On the wall behind him was a large flag with NER embroidered in black on the cross of St George.

"Welcome, especially to our new members. The NER is growing. This country's falling apart. Immigrants, blacks, asylum seekers, they're not escaping war – they just want to come over here and take what's ours. We've just opened the doors to more. Bulgarians and Romanians, they're not like us. These people from Africa."

A voice called out, "Send them back." And, "Let them drown."

Tyler nodded. "We English are suffering. People are losing hope; they can't get jobs and kids are going hungry.

We're offering an alternative, get rid of those that don't belong here then there'll be plenty for the rest of us." People were nodding and murmuring. "Right, next up we've got some people here tonight who've been on the frontline and want to tell their stories."

A big bloke got up. He talked about standing up to a gang of black thugs who were harassing a white girl. Said they jumped on him and he was in hospital for weeks with a ruptured spleen. He got a big cheer. Then the woman sitting near me stood up. She had long red hair and a tight-fitting dress. She was spreading the word about the NER on her housing estate, got some shit from people but she kept going. She'd already recruited three people.

A sad-looking middle-aged bloke spoke last. "My kid got killed in Iraq last year." A murmur of sympathy went round the room. "He went out to do a job and got murdered by one of them, someone who was meant to be on his side. That's the thanks he got. I went to pieces for a bit then I decided to do something instead. That's why I'm here."

Tyler stood up. "Thanks, the three of you. These stories are just a small part of what's going on. It's time for some action. We're sick of having our hands tied by that bitch of a Home Secretary. Every time we plan a big demo she blocks it so instead we're going to try a new tactic. I'm forming some small action groups who will be sent to different areas of London and appear without warning. That way we keep reminding people we're here to stay. Those of you who want to be involved stay behind at the end."

I liked what I was hearing. These people were speaking straight to me and they were out there trying to change things, even the women. I wanted to be part of it so I stayed behind.

Tyler said, "This new campaign needs to stay between us for now, no bragging to friends or girlfriends about what we're doing. We need to stop the enemy or the press getting hold of it."

He divided us into small groups. I was with Chris and two other blokes; Billy, the one whose kid had been killed and a geezer called Luke. Chris was named as leader of our group. Tyler told us what we'd be doing but not when; that information would be given to Chris first who'd text us closer to the time. It was like being involved in a secret military organisation. When we'd got our instructions we went down to the bar. People were telling stories about stuff they'd done.

Billy told us about the RNO, another group he'd been involved in.

"The bloke in charge kept putting his foot in it, couldn't handle the media, it was getting embarrassing. He even started talking to Muslims. That's when I left and joined the NER. I prefer it. Tyler knows what he's talking about."

"What brings you here, mate?" Luke said to me.

"A gang of them mugged my girlfriend, stole her phone and roughed her up, she's suffering from trauma now."

It was the first thing that came into my head. I didn't want him to know I'd been scared.

Then I told him about the beggar and the accordion. "He won't be playing again, I smashed that fucking box thing to pieces."

"Well done, sounds like you're on a mission."

It was the best time I'd had for ages, like having a big family of people who all thought the same as I did.

6

VALERIE

I made the most of two free days and went to Sheffield. Anton met me at the station and we caught a bus to his place. In a cafe round the corner we ordered coffee and cake.

"Here's to us, our first professional parts," he said, clinking his mug against mine.

"I can't believe I'm going to have a real audience who've paid to be there. I'm on stage as often as Richard. It's going to be intense."

For a moment I wondered if I could do it. Anton must have seen my expression because he said, "You'll be fine, Valerie, I've got faith in you."

Later that evening I took my seat near the front of the stalls. When Anton first came on stage I was nervous for him but as soon as he began to sing I knew it would be OK. His voice was rich and low and he held the stage as if he'd been doing it for years. I watched his face and could see how much he was enjoying himself. He'd made the transition from acting student to actor with ease; perhaps I could do it too.

It was snowing when we came out of the theatre. A few

centimetres already lay on the pavement and cars. Thinking that the bus might not make it up the hill we started walking back to his flat, our shoes crunching in the dry crispness. I watched as the thick flakes caught in his hair. He bent down and scooped up a ball and threw it at me. I grabbed a fistful and hurled it back and soon we were covered in snow.

"Stop!" I said, laughing. "That one went down my neck, it was freezing."

He stopped and we linked arms and walked, slipping and sliding slowly up the steep hill to his flat. We stayed up late talking. It was like being at college again but better because now we had real roles to talk about. Later he said, "I'll sleep in here and you have the bed."

Through a curtain was a small room with just enough space for a double bed and his clothes. It was organised and tidy, a rail of coloured shirts and shoes neatly stowed underneath. I had a shower in the tiny bathroom that had the smallest basin I'd ever seen. He kissed me goodnight. What he'd said about him and Leila and that it might not work out came back to my mind and I didn't look at him full on in case my confusion showed. Lying in bed I was aware of him in the other room, so close I could almost hear him breathing.

* * *

Rehearsals lasted for seven weeks. I wanted more time but Lucy said I was ready. We were given our costumes for the dress rehearsal. In the first scene I was wearing a short, flowered dress. I'd never have chosen it in real life but I knew it was right for Chrissie. When Richard, who'd become Paul, walked on stage in his army uniform for the first time, for a moment I thought he really had come back from a war.

As the first night grew nearer I dreamt about being on stage. Sometimes the audience looked happy. Other times strange things happened. Once a crow flew onto the stage in the middle of an important scene. It strutted around pecking at imaginary food. Another time I found Richard backstage with blood pouring from a wound in his leg.

On the morning of the first night I did no more preparation. I went to the cafe in the nearby park. It was a cold, sunny day and the frost on the ground hadn't yet melted. I drank coffee and ate a croissant and imagined I was a tourist in Paris or Berlin who had nothing particular to do that day.

The curtain opened. I was on stage alone, waiting for Paul to return from a night out. I stood looking out at the audience, holding their collective gaze. A moment later he entered. He was looking for ways to escape what was happening in his mind and I was trying to cope with his moods. All the time we were waiting for a letter saying 'You are being posted to …' When it came, he pretended he was sorry but we both knew he wasn't sorry at all.

The first act flowed and before I knew it the interval came. I changed my costume, had time to drink some water and exchange a few words with Karen, who was playing Paul's sister, then we started again. At the end of the play I was left on stage alone and began Chrissie's monologue.

"You're glad to be going back to where you can feel something, not living with me where there are no shells overhead, no landmines, no comrades to hold your breath with as you lurch over the next lump in the road, no one who shares your terror. Only me, Chrissie, who wants you, but as you used to be, not as you are now."

I could sense the tension and there was complete silence in the audience. No lines were missed, no props failed, no lights refused to come on.

As the curtain came down I stood between Richard and Karen ready to take our bows, feeling completely present and alive. Dad came into my head but for once it didn't make me sad; I sensed that he was there, applauding.

Outside Mum and Keri were waiting for me, along with Renee and Bridget, my friend from school.

Bridget said, "I always knew you'd do brilliantly, ever since Hermia."

* * *

Back at the flat I picked up the photo of Dad, who was standing with his arms folded, smiling, as if he was pleased with me. He was the one who started my love of it all. When I was little he told me stories, African folk tales, English fairy stories, sometimes combining the two, sitting next to the bed, his face illuminated by the lamp, which had pictures of giraffes and elephants on the shade. Sometimes the stories were too scary and I squealed. Mum came into the room to see what the noise was.

"She'll never get to sleep, Joseph."

My head was full of goblins, elves, African spirits and princesses, all mixed into one. I started making up my own stories, inventing characters and plots and getting my friends to act them out. Sometimes I surprised Mum and Dad by jumping out from behind the door.

"The Scorpion King sends you good wishes," I said, with a bow.

Once I overheard Mum whispering to Dad. "She lives in a world of her own."

"She is fine, she has a good imagination, that's all," he said.

At school I found most of the lessons boring and often got told off for whispering to Bridget. When I was twelve I started doing drama. The tutor, Ms Anderson, didn't seem to mind me talking. She said, "You're very curious, Valerie, that's a great thing in life."

At first we read plays that were hard and cold, full of angry people. I started to wish I hadn't chosen it but then in the spring term we began *A Midsummer Night's Dream* and I was caught up in the world of Shakespeare for the first time. Ms Anderson said there'd be a performance at the end of the year and I let out an excited yelp, which made everyone laugh.

She told us to think about which part we wanted to play because instead of holding auditions she was going to try to let everyone have their chosen role. We wrote down our first, second and third choice on a sheet of paper and gave it to her. She hoped everyone would get their first or second choice. I knew straight away I wanted to be Hermia. I already had an idea of how I might perform her.

The room was buzzing. Bridget said she wanted to play Titania. Sarah turned round and said, "You'll get that part," then she said to Debbie, loudly enough for me to hear, "Everyone knows Hermia's got blonde hair and she's really pretty, so Valerie can't play her."

My head jerked, as if someone had slapped me across

the face really hard. I could hear the certainty and hate in her voice. Tears came into my eyes.

Bridget looked at me and whispered, "We should tell Ms Anderson what she said."

I shook my head. I wouldn't let anyone else see how much it hurt. I put my head down and squeezed the tears back inside.

Later Ms Anderson read out the list of names and parts.

"Bridget is playing Titania. Valerie is playing Hermia."

I wanted her to say it again to make sure I hadn't misheard. Bridget said, "Yes" loudly. At break we tried acting out our parts in the playground, celebrating. I caught the look of disgust on Sarah's face but I knew I'd won.

From then on I spent hours in my room rehearsing and Mum had to almost drag me out to eat. Sometimes Keri came in to listen, sitting on the edge of the bed with her legs swinging. She always clapped in the wrong place.

Ms Anderson made adjustments to the play so it was shorter but I still had some long speeches.

"My good Lysander! I swear to thee, by Cupid's strongest bow…" The lines came easily, I learnt how to move, how to become Hermia. Gordon was playing Lysander. He was Scottish and sometimes people teased him because of his strong accent but I thought it sounded nice.

Two days before the performance we were given our costumes. Mine was a long blue dress and a hairband covered in pink and white flowers. Bridget was in white with yellow flowers. Mum said I looked beautiful which made me cry.

The evening passed really quickly. We all remembered our lines, even Debbie and Maya, who always forgot them in rehearsals. I couldn't believe how exciting it was, everyone in costume and make-up, with proper lighting. I loved being in the centre of the stage, when I was speaking and everyone else was quiet.

Mum, Dad and Keri were all there. Afterwards everyone, all the teachers and parents, gathered around.

Dad said, "Of course Valerie was the real star," a bit too loudly.

"Ssh, Dad, you can't say that," I hissed.

Ms Anderson turned to us and said, "You did very well, Valerie. You could think of choosing drama as a career."

I already had. This was my world, dressing up, being part of something that put a spell on people.

Soon after that Dad died. I came home from school one day and Grandma opened the door. She said in a serious voice, "Come and be with your mother, Valerie."

Mum was sitting on the sofa crying. Keri was clinging to her. They said there'd been an accident at work. Dad had been killed when something fell on him. An accident. The words about him not coming back didn't make sense. He always came back. I didn't remember much after that. Sometimes at night I heard Mum crying. I missed Dad so much I got pains in my stomach. I missed him hugging me when he got in from work. Most of all I missed his stories.

I studied his face in the photo, shut my eyes and listened for his voice. He said, "I knew you could do it Valerie, I always had faith in you." I wasn't going to let him or myself down. I was going to make the most of this chance.

7

JIMMY

Next day Chris, Billy, Luke and me met at the station. On the Tube people looked at us then turned away. I drew myself up, feeling good. Our destination was Walthamstow, meeting place, a small park. Another group was already there. Chris went over and spoke to a tall, thin bloke in a baseball cap. When he came back he said, "So far no one's got wind of what we're doing. Soon as they do they'll call the cops. If it kicks off you have my permission to defend yourselves. Any way you like."

Adrenaline was running through me. I buttoned my jacket, ready.

"We're going to move towards the target. When we get to the end of this road we fan out. Our group heads for Market Road, the others go down Claremont Street. That puts us at either end of the high street then we start marching towards each other. Make as much noise as you can. The aim is to intimidate."

We walked past rows of terraced houses with weird symbols hanging in the windows. The main street was full of Pakis, going about their lives as if they owned the place. We pulled our flags out from our coats and lifted them up, a sea of red and white, and began chanting, "England for Whites. Pakis and blacks go home. No Sharia law. Repatriation now."

People were turning to stare. Women held onto their children and moved out of our way. A group of men in white dresses and lace hats were walking up the road; we stood in a line blocking them. They tried to push through us but we stood our ground. They moved to one side and we blocked them.

"Piss off man. What the fuck are you doing?" one of them said.

"This is our country, we don't want your laws here," I said.

"We don't want racists in this borough," another one said.

He started pushing up his sleeves and I saw the muscles in his arms. Fear jumped into my throat.

I yelled, "Fuck off," and he took a swing at me, he missed and I ran at him, throwing all my weight against him. He lost his footing, fell into the road and a car had to swerve to avoid him. Out of the corner of my eye I saw Chris fighting with someone. All around was shouting. Horns sounded. It was mad. I hit another in the stomach and saw the shock on his face. Someone hurled a bottle and it hit one of the Pakis on the side of the head. I saw blood coming down. It was like a war. A fist came at me, I tried to dodge it but felt a sharp blow in my ribs and the next thing I knew I was on the pavement. I pulled myself up, dazed. Chris was kicking a man on the ground.

At that moment I heard sirens and saw blue flashing lights at the end of the street.

Chris shouted, "Run," and we scattered. I followed him

down a side street. When we got far enough away we slowed down.

"Fucking hell, did you see their faces? They were scared as shit," I said, panting.

"I hammered one of them in his gut, he won't be eating any curry tonight," Chris said, laughing his head off.

We were pumped up and triumphant, joking and messing about on the way back to south-east London. We met up with the others at the pub. There was stuff on the local news about the disturbances; the Home Secretary saying it was unacceptable. We heard that Luke and another geezer had been arrested – they'd gone the wrong way down one of the streets and bumped into the police.

"Collateral damage. Anyway, they'll probably get off with a caution. We did a good job," Chris said, downing his pint and calling for another.

It was after midnight when we left. We hung around outside for a while smoking and congratulating each other. We walked back to the estate. For once I didn't notice what a shithole I was living in.

* * *

Tyler's right-hand man was arrested on a charge of inciting racial hatred. It was bollocks of course – all he was doing was defending our rights but it meant that Tyler started relying on Chris and me more. I'd never had any power in my life and now the boss of the NER thought I was someone.

Ten of us were meeting in our usual place, just the people that Tyler most trusted. There was something he wanted to discuss but we had to make sure no one else heard about it. The AF – Anti-Fascists – were always on our case. They were mad and fearless. They were good at surveillance and infiltration so we had to be on our toes.

Tyler said, "This spineless government is trying to box us in but I've got ideas about how to proceed."

He took a drink of orange juice. He never drank alcohol, said he needed to keep a clear mind for the battles ahead.

"I want you to organise a flash mob, film it and put it on YouTube; we need to use social media to spread the word. So long as it isn't illegal we can do what we like. Free speech in this country. Tell the membership there'll be an event soon then give two hours' notice on the day. That way we're less likely to get stopped. Chris and Jimmy, you're in charge."

Chris was sitting in front. He turned and nodded at me.

"Make a banner and hang it where a lot of people will see it. I'll give you the slogan and you organise the time and place. Get as many together as you can."

People started talking. Tyler held his hand up.

"This is a small, though important, action. I'm planning something bigger. Some of our brothers and sisters are coming over from Scandinavia. They've got strong networks there. I want to learn from them. We need to find ways of closing our borders. The Border Agency is letting people in under the radar. The Tories and UKIP are all talk but they don't change anything."

He paused for a moment. Things were getting serious now. The thought of meeting a group from abroad was exciting.

"I'm in contact with the main man from Norway. We're discussing time and place. I'll get back to you when I know more. Get on with organising the flash mob."

I bought two cans of black spray paint and Chris got a white sheet off his mum. We met up in a garage belonging to a mate. Chris said my writing was better than his so I was doing the work. Tyler told us the slogan he wanted us to use, 'Diversity is White Genocide'. That would get people talking. I planned out the lettering in my mind though when I did it I had to make the letters of 'Genocide' smaller to fit in the space. Still, it looked good.

8

VALERIE

One night Anton came to see *Wounded Home*. I could sense his presence and it seemed to give my whole performance more meaning.

Afterwards in the bar he said, "You've got Chrissie, she's totally believable. I loved that scene where it's just you and the mirror."

He'd always been honest about what he thought so I was really pleased. We chatted about the play and the other performances. Later he told me he'd had another row with Leila and this time their relationship was over. Surrounded by music and noise I couldn't decide what I felt. When we left the bar he said he was heading back to his dad's place. We walked to the Tube.

At the entrance I said, without thinking about the future, "Come back with me for a while, so we can go on talking."

For an instant I thought I was being too forward, too pushy, but he said, "I was hoping you might say that."

Back at the flat we stood in silence looking out of the window. The branches on the trees stretched up and out like country lanes on a map.

I went into the kitchen, took two mugs from the

cupboard and placed them side by side. A tall green one and a wider blue one. I studied them. The blue didn't seem right so I put it back and took out the other green one. I put coffee in both and waited for the kettle to boil. I leant against the sink and pointed the toes of one foot out in front of the other, like a ballet dancer would do. What did I want? I poured water into the mugs. The milk was nearly finished. I divided it between us. I was certain that 'a while' was what I meant when I suggested it, but now? I shut my eyes and thought I felt his lips brush my cheek.

We were at each end of the sofa, not breaching the unspoken boundary. The pattern on the fabric seemed more pronounced than usual, orange circles and crimson spirals on a dark background. I liked it when I first moved in. My hand rested on it. The fingernails were painted silver; the varnish on my little finger was just beginning to chip. Was it too soon? Would we spoil what was good and precious?

Looking at him I took in his face, wide cheekbones and mouth, his long neck, the turquoise shirt open at the top, small curls of black hair showing.

I want him. That was the thought in its purest form. It was like a perfect globe, a new marble, with no bumps or imperfections. Nothing could disturb it and it would not be denied. I placed the globe between us and spoke its thoughts.

"Will you stay?"

It hung suspended for a moment then he spoke.

"Yes."

It was all that needed to be said.

We looked at each other and I could see it was the right moment after all.

He put his hand against my cheek; I could feel the warm roughness of his palm. I put my lips on his. They were smooth and cool.

He was familiar and unfamiliar, I knew him and I didn't. I knew the shape of his body clothed but when he revealed it, it was surprising, captivating. Strong arm and thigh muscles, a compact frame over longer legs.

Sometimes, with other boyfriends, I'd felt shy with my own nakedness but now was different. I took off my clothes and fitted myself against him. There was time, time to notice everything and to feel how it was. The window was open at the top; I felt a breath of air move across my back. I put my cheek against his, hands under his shoulders, breasts pressed against his chest. When I looked closely his eyes had flecks of gold amongst the dark brown, his hair had grown in the last year and was starting to twist into shapes. I curled my fingers into them and around them. His hands were across my back, palms flat, pulling me in, enclosing me.

He said, "This is how it should be, this close. You are just right. Don't go away from me."

Outside someone laughed. Inside we breathed deeply, I breathed in what he meant. I took in his thoughts. He breathed on my hot skin, "You and me, Valerie. Us."

The night passed. Sometimes we slept. We didn't let go of each other. There was an arm against an arm, a cheek against a chest, a hand resting on the inner curve of a thigh. A quietness after a passion.

In the morning we ate breakfast, sharing the last three pieces of toast, the coffee with no milk. I wanted to say something, something about the night but I couldn't shape it into the right words, so instead I told funny stories, watching him laugh, wriggling in his chair at my ridiculousness.

He said he had to go but he'd be back as soon as he could.

"I'll see you then?" he said in an urgent, worried tone as if he was afraid I might say no.

* * *

A part of me knew I'd fall in love. We were hovering on the brink and that felt right.

One day I was in Oxford. I passed a small designer shop on a side street and went in. I looked around, searching for the right thing. There were shirts on a rail, lemon yellow, purple, green, all of which would look good on him. Then at the side a mannequin caught my eye, it was clothed in black, around its throat was a scarf. Pink and orange stripes that swirled downwards, elegant, flamboyant, joyous. When I touched it I knew it was silk.

The young woman wrapped it in tissue and smiled when she handed it to me.

I put it in a padded envelope with a postcard from the Tate Gallery, a painting by Matisse of a view from a window. I wrote, 'When I saw this I knew it was yours. Valerie xx.' I posted the scarf and walked home across the park; pink light was glinting through the trees, streetlamps were flickering on one by one. I was smiling to myself, wondering how long the parcel would take to arrive, imagining him opening it.

When he called he said, "It's perfect, the colours are beautiful. I'll wear it when I next see you."

The next two weeks went by in a blur. If I didn't think

about it three days went by. Other times I sat and looked at the clock waiting for a minute to pass. I hardly needed to sleep. I floated through performances. Renee said, "You seem different. Is it the play? It must be good for you."

"Yes, I suppose it is," I said.

I hadn't told anyone about Anton. Usually I couldn't keep secrets but this was so new, so fragile, I didn't want anyone to say, "But hasn't he just split up with Leila, isn't it too soon?"

* * *

The few weeks run of *Wounded Home* passed quickly and it was soon to finish. I would miss the other actors and Chrissie, who'd become part of my life. There were reviews in the local papers. One I was really proud of – 'In her first role, Valerie Wilding puts in a performance that is both powerful and nuanced.'

I thought I'd remember those few weeks forever, the time of my first play and becoming close to Anton. I couldn't say it was the first time I'd been in love. I'd had other boyfriends who I'd loved but it was the first time the passion had linked up with something else, a deeper connection, a sense of being on the same road.

Anton's run had finished too and he texted to say he was coming for the whole weekend. He was arriving on Thursday, he had something to do that evening but he'd come round on the Friday. I couldn't wait to see him.

The flat was a mess so I changed the sheets and smoothed out the patchwork bedspread, which I'd made from pieces of African fabric that I collected from markets.

I was ridiculously proud of it. I put the mugs and plates away and dusted the plant on the windowsill. I looked out across the park. There'd been a thick frost in the night and the grass was still wet. Two men were walking towards the gate, hands in their pockets, deep in conversation. There was something about them that I didn't like the look of, a thrust of a fist, the swagger of the one on the right. I turned away.

9

JIMMY

Two hours before the action we sent a text to our members. 'Footbridge A13 4.30.' We picked up the banner and placards and headed for the meeting place.

About twenty others turned up. There was loads of traffic on the road below and we started attaching the banner to the railings of the bridge. When Chris gave us the thumbs-up we unfurled it. Someone was filming from the side. The black letters on the white sheet looked brilliant. We could see people in cars looking up as they went underneath. We were definitely getting our message across. Some hooted and one passenger unwound his window and gave a thumbs-up.

We'd been there for about an hour when a cop car arrived. The two blokes that got out were friendly and there was no threat of arrest just a polite, "move along now folks, some people have complained about your message," so we pulled up the banner and told them we were on our way. Job done. A group of us headed back to the pub to celebrate. Billy got the first round in.

The TV was on and someone was saying that the leader of a far right party in Ukraine had been allowed into the

UK. Tyler talked about him as if he was something special. He believed that gypsies should be put in ghettos and that Jews were part of a conspiracy and that he had a lot of power in his own country. We crowded round to watch the TV, which showed him giving a speech. Protestors had tried to stop him by blocking the Tube station but his supporters had arranged a second location and he spoke uninterrupted.

We cheered when we heard that and drank a toast to the new white England.

Billy and the others left the pub first. Chris and me stood outside for a while smoking, draining our pints, cigarettes glowing, Chris telling crude jokes. Our laughter flipped up and echoed off the block of flats opposite. The atmosphere was loose. We were ready, like fighting dogs on a leash.

* * *

A man on the other side of the road was looking at us. As I watched he slipped something in his pocket and walked away. Chris was finishing his pint.

"There was someone over the road, a nigger, he had a camera," I said.

"Which way did he go?"

I pointed to a narrow street.

"You sure he was taking photos?"

"Yeah."

"Let's get after him then."

We left the pub and crossed the road, walking close together. On one side of the street was a high wall with barbed wire curled along the top. We passed large shuttered gates – at the end of the road was a gasworks – huge and dark. He was about a hundred yards away. At a junction he crossed and went straight ahead. We followed silently. We were catching up then Chris coughed. He turned and saw us and began to run.

Up ahead was a line of trees. We were near the common. He crossed another road and ran straight into it along a diagonal path. He was quick but I was a good sprinter. He took a look back, saw me catching up and broke off to the right across the grass. I increased my pace, lungs filling up, pushing harder. Chris couldn't keep up so it was down to me.

I was getting close. I made a grab for his arm but he pulled it away and changed direction, heading for an area of trees. There was no way I was letting him escape. I was going to get that camera. He ducked under a branch and I followed. All I could hear was our breathing; his was loud and desperate. He stumbled over a log and I sprang forward.

"Give me the fucking phone!" I shouted.

His face was marked with fear and anger. He threw a punch at my chest but missed, he turned to run but Chris had caught up and was blocking his path. The man put his fists up.

"Leave me alone," he screamed.

Chris sneered, teeth showing through thick lips. I crouched, ready for a move. He broke away and tried to run out of the trees but Chris and me moved together and caught him. A streetlamp was flickering on and off, illuminating him. Chris pulled something from his pocket. I caught a glimpse of the drawn blade just before it entered his body, under his ribs.

"What?" I said.

"Shut up," Chris said, straightening up and darting a look around. The knife was in his right hand. There was blood on it. The man on the ground was groaning. His face was in shadow.

"That's done him. I've got the phone, go," Chris said. I thought about an ambulance but Chris was already running.

At the gate he hissed, "I'm turning right, go the other way."

* * *

Turning left I started walking, not knowing where I was going. When I thought I'd gone far enough I sat in an empty bus shelter. My breathing was choppy as if the air was too thin. I saw the knife – a six-inch long blade and Chris's expression, which was one of intent.

I looked at my hands – the fingers looked like bones, as if the flesh had shrunk away. There were grey hairs on my jacket, I touched my head and felt thinness at the temples. I turned into an old man who remembered the knife. I shook my head trying to clear the vision but instead I saw him lying on his back under the bushes, one hand stretched out, pink palm turned upwards, blood seeping from his body into the dead leaves.

A bus drew up, but I didn't get on. A couple came and stood in the shelter so I started walking. I saw a street name and realised I'd been down it already and was heading back to the common. I turned and went the other way. I came to a station and got on a train to New Cross. The woman opposite kept looking at me warily as if I might pounce on her or something. I stared at the floor. I didn't want anyone fixing my face in their mind.

When I got back the house was dark. I knew I should wash my clothes but I couldn't put the machine on without waking Mum. I went up to my room, took off my jeans and got into bed. I lay there trying to understand what'd just happened. One minute we were telling jokes in a pub then Chris was stabbing a man.

I shut my eyes and tried to wipe away the images of the chase and the park. Maybe I'd imagined it like when I was young and drew a picture of Wayne with a knife in his heart. I made the shape and coloured it in. The blade of the knife was black and there were drops of red blood coming from the wound. His arms were up and his mouth was open. I hoped that if I drew it well enough I could make it happen.

10

VALERIE

Kora music was playing. I fumbled for my mobile.

"Are you awake?" Renee's voice sounded distorted. The clock said 6.30 a.m.

I pushed the phone closer to my ear. "What is it?"

"Matthew just phoned."

I pictured him – tall, white, hair all over the place. He talked a lot and was involved in some political organisation.

"What about?"

"It's Anton," she interrupted.

An atom of fear fluttered in my chest.

"What's happened?"

"I can't…"

"What?" I said, insistent.

"He was attacked last night."

Shock flowed through my veins like a piece of wire. Everything stopped, my breathing, traffic, the wind in the trees.

"Oh God."

My hand went to the side of the bed where he was meant to be soon.

"Is he alright?"

"I'm so sorry, Matthew said he was taken to hospital but he died."

The words were like a flash explosion. Light from the streetlamp turned ice white. A sound emerged like a howl. I dropped the phone on the floor. From far away I could hear Renee's voice calling, "Valerie, are you OK?"

The cold of the room surrounded me.

"He can't be dead."

I wanted to hurl the phone at the wall.

"Sorry, it's terrible."

"What happened, who did… who was it?"

"I don't know; do you want Matthew's number? You could talk to him."

She said she'd text me the number and call me later.

I got out of bed, my body shaking and teeth chattering, picking up my jumper from the floor. I pulled it on but it didn't stop the shaking. Holding my stomach I walked round and round the flat, retching sobs coming from deep inside.

In the kitchen I took out a mug, the one he'd drunk from, imagining I could still feel the warmth of his hand. Keeping hold of it I went to the window and looked out, wanting to believe he was still alive and on his way to see me.

In the park a low white mist hovered over the ground. No one rang the bell. At last I picked up the phone and dialled Matthew's number.

A voice said, "Hello."

"I'm Valerie, a friend…"

"I know who you are, we've met."

"Is it true?" A second passed and I felt a rush of hope.

"Yes." There.

I pressed the disconnect button.

* * *

In the photo taken at the showcase Anton and me had our arms round each other and we were smiling. His face was alive and full of hope. I remembered the feeling of his breath on my neck and his words in my ear. I wanted to kill whoever had killed him. To make them feel like I did, to hurt them, to twist their balls and put a gun to their head. I wanted to blind them and shout obscenities, tear out their fingernails.

I pulled a pillow onto the floor and curled up, crying into it, "I can't lose him, please, I can't lose him," over and over again until I was exhausted, then lay holding the photo to my chest. At some point I must have slept.

Renee called again. I told her about Anton and me. "I always knew you two should be together. It's tragic."

Was that all there was? I had him for a passing moment and then the light went out.

Matthew phoned in the afternoon and said if I went over he'd tell me what he knew. There was nothing else to do. I should have been with Anton; instead I was going to talk to someone about how he died. I got dressed, pulling on as many layers as I could. It was meant to be spring but winter wouldn't let go.

Matthew lived in a block of flats in New Cross. When he came to the door we stood awkwardly for a moment. Then he said, "Come in. Do you want some coffee?"

I nodded, not because I did but because it would make things seem normal.

The living room was strewn with papers and piles of magazines, some still in packages.

"Have a seat," he said, sweeping stuff off a chair.

Coming back from the kitchen he put a mug in front of me and sat opposite. He tried to smile but it faded quickly.

"I need to know what happened," I said, clenching my hands in front of me as if to protect myself from whatever he was going to say.

"Someone found him in a park, he was injured and they called an ambulance. They tried to save him but he died in hospital."

I looked down, trying to keep the tears in and failing.

"I'm really sorry," he said.

"Do they know who…?" It was a pointless question; they never knew immediately, sometimes they never knew at all.

He shook his head. "I haven't heard anymore than that. They'll only tell his family."

I thought about his dad who I'd met once and his brother who I hadn't.

"Did you know Anton was getting involved in the AF?" he said.

I looked up. "Who's that?"

"Anti-Fascists, I'm a member too."

I shook my head. I knew he'd seen Matthew recently but I thought they were just friends.

"We got word about some new activity in the NER, that's the New English Right, something more sinister than their usual stuff. We think they were meeting last night. I saw Anton earlier and we discussed monitoring. We have a rule that anything we do is in twos or threes, nothing on your own. Later I got a call from someone who said there'd been an attack on one of our members and found out it was Anton."

He talked really fast and it was hard to take in what he was saying. I needed to ask how he died and braced myself for the blow.

"How…?"

He stood up abruptly and went to the window. I watched his back. His wavy hair stood out like a dark halo. His shoulders drooped. When he swung round I could see there were tears in his eyes.

"He was stabbed I think. I don't know much more than that. It's terrible."

I put my hands over my face. I wanted to scream.

"He was found on the common. Maybe he was taking a short cut to the Tube."

All I could think was that I wasn't there with him.

"We were meant to be seeing each other this weekend."

"Were you in a relationship?"

"We'd been friends for ages and when he split up with Leila, we…" I stood up. "I have to go," though going meant being alone.

* * *

The next morning I woke early with a sense of dread, the air around me seemed to be permeated by a heavy mist. I got up and dressed in my black top and leggings. I was meant to be starting work again at the cafe but when I tried to open the flat door it felt like a dead weight. Walking slowly back to the bedroom I took off my jacket, sat on the bed and cried.

I stayed in the bedroom all that day – sleeping and waking, looking at the outline of the window and the light coming in around the edges of the curtains. Renee called to see if I wanted her to come round but I said no. Mum begged me to come over and have a meal with her but I told her I didn't want to eat. I needed to let the grief drown me and pierce me, enter every pore. I wanted to remember all the things we'd done and imagine all the things we'd never do. I needed to hold onto him, cradle him, while I could still remember what it was like to be close.

11

JIMMY

A car alarm pierced my sleep. For a second it was just another day then I remembered. We were drinking – there was a fight – Chris stabbed someone.

I jumped out of bed, opened the laptop and clicked on the news. Man attacked on common dies in hospital. Died, dying, DEAD. I stared at the words, unable to move, until the screen went black.

We were in deep shit. I was in deep shit. Chris was a fucking maniac. My heart was pounding and I felt sick. I had to think and quick. I listened at the bedroom door – Mum was moving around downstairs. Waiting until I heard her go out, I grabbed the clothes I'd been wearing the night before, ran downstairs and shoved them in the machine. Then I had a shower, as hot as I could stand, using the last of the soap. Back in my room I stood looking out at the estate. The long grey blocks stared back. I could hear a siren on the main road and wondered if it was heading my way.

I replayed the scene in my mind – could see the man running, hear the sound of his breathing. I saw him fall, heard him groan. It was over so quick, one blow, that's all it took. I lit a fag, my fingers shaking. I had to talk to Chris and figure out how to get our story straight. I thought about CCTV. We weren't wearing hoods – we could easily have been picked up on cameras. I didn't have previous but Chris did. He got done for beating up his brother's mate who was a queer. He did nine months for that. I hated the police, worse was the idea of being locked in a cell, no way out.

There was a war going on between us English and the immigrants, between white and black. People died in wars. Plus he was taking photos of us and we had a right to stop it. We could say it was self-defence and he went for us first. Who was to say any different? For a split second the image of the man's upturned palm appeared in my mind. I shook my head trying to clear the vision. I needed to keep things normal. Get to work.

I was pulling on my clothes then thought of something. The man had been wearing something pink, what was it? I stopped dressing to think. It was round his neck, it was a scarf, like a woman's. By the time we got to the trees it had gone. It must have come off when we were running or when I first made a grab for him. I remembered feeling something soft. If I'd touched it, my DNA would be on it. I lit another fag, trying to hold back the fear flooding through my body then I called Chris.

He picked up after a couple of rings and hissed, "Don't call me, I'll meet you later."

I paced round the room, trying to work out what to do. I had to find that scarf. There'd be cops crawling all over the place by now but I'd have to risk it.

I made myself a coffee and sat in the kitchen, telling myself I could do it. Liam came in, yawning.

"Alright? You up for fishing again this weekend?" he

said, sounding like he didn't have a clue what was going on, which he didn't.

"Sorry mate, too busy."

"Suit yourself," he said and shrugged.

Before he could say anything else I went out the door. I was back at the common in half an hour. It was raining. A police van was parked near the main entrance and I could see stuff happening in the distance. I watched for a while trying to decide if I could get away with it. It started raining harder. There was CCTV on a lamp post but I couldn't see any in the park. A black man walked past. I avoided his eye and began walking along the diagonal path trying to act casual, shifting my mouth into a position that didn't look guilty.

As I got closer to where it happened I could see people clustered around, some were wearing white suits. A large area was taped off. If he'd dropped the scarf there I was stuffed. Paths went in several directions. I tried to remember which way we'd gone. He'd run all over the place trying to shake us off. There was an area of trees and shrubs to the right. I moved slowly towards it, trying not to draw attention to myself. No one spotted me so I darted in. As I pushed through the branches a bunch of wet leaves hit me in the face. Cursing I started searching the ground but there was no sign of the scarf.

Closer to where the police were was another group of trees. I didn't think I'd get away with it but I had no choice so I headed across the grass. I was halfway there when someone from the crime scene started coming towards me. I froze, not knowing whether to keep walking or turn and run. After another gut-wrenching moment the person turned back and, with my heart pounding, I ducked into the trees. I scanned the ground, more and more desperate, then seeing a flash of colour I made a grab for it. It was the scarf, covered in grass. I crushed it into a ball and shoved it in my pocket. Pushing my way through the branches to the other side I looked out; there was no one around so I walked quickly away. Reaching the road I zipped my pocket up tight.

* * *

"You're late," Ray said.

"Sorry."

I needed to stay on the right side of him, so I got to work on the living room straight away. Ray was in the hall, whistling along to the radio. The news came on and I stopped painting and listened intently. Right at the end the voice said that the police were investigating the death of a man attacked on the common. I missed my footing on the stepladder and a blob of cream paint dripped onto the slate fireplace. I climbed down, grabbed a cloth and wiped it off. Ray didn't stop whistling.

I wanted to talk to Shelley but knew I was going to have to make it sound better than it did – 'I was just trying to get him to delete the photos, I didn't mean anything by it, Chris is a fucking idiot,' but she didn't always agree with me about things; in fact recently she'd started defending some illegals, saying she thought people were giving them a hard time. She might not be sympathetic.

At lunchtime Ray said, "You alright Jimmy? You're looking a bit pale."

"Got a headache, that's all," I said, trying to sound calm.

He found me an aspirin and I felt bad because he was being sympathetic. Somehow I made it through the day.

At home I went straight to my room and took the scarf out of my pocket. I looked at it closely. Even though I'd crunched it into a tight ball it wasn't creased. There was a small smudge of green on the corner but no other incriminating evidence. It was long with wavy stripes, pink and orange. I looked at the label, 100% pure silk. What was a man doing wearing that?

I couldn't put it in the bin in case mum saw it so I folded it up and put it back in my pocket. I'd get rid of it later.

At 8 p.m. Chris texted, 'usual place now.'

"You keeping quiet, Jimmy?"

He looked like his normal self but there was an edge to his voice.

"Act normal. Get an alibi, as soon as. I'm sorted. There's this girl – she's been trying to get me to shag her for weeks, I've promised her everything she wants. She's not bad as it happens, she'll swear blind I was with her all night. And you didn't see me, right?"

He took a puff of his fag. It was hard to believe he'd just killed someone. He could convince anyone of anything. He'd covered himself but what about me? I couldn't think of a single soul who would help.

"Mum and Liam were in bed when I got home."

"You better find someone. What about Shelley?"

I knew he was going to say her before he said it. I also knew that I wasn't going to ask her.

Luckily he didn't wait for my answer. "We can't meet up again, don't want the old bill seeing us together, plus the NER don't want loose cannons. They'll be happy about what we achieved but they won't take the rap."

He smiled. It wasn't a friendly smile. He was trying to make out it was as much my fault as his.

"Right, go then," he said. He was lighting another fag, big hands cupping the flame.

I walked back through the estate. Rain was slanting between the tower blocks. Large puddles were collecting at the bottom of the stairwells. By the time I reached the flat door I felt like I was drowning.

I was putting the key in the lock when I remembered I hadn't got rid of the scarf. I started back down the stairs. At the bottom I bumped into Shelley. She didn't look happy.

"Where were you last night? You didn't answer your phone."

There'd been a missed call from her, must have been around the time we were in the park.

"I was down the pub, I didn't hear it, sorry."

"Who were you with?"

I couldn't say Chris because I wasn't meant to have seen him.

"The usual, you know, Ian and Danny," I said, trying to sound casual.

"Not Chris then?"

"No, he was out with some girl."

She flashed me a look like she didn't believe me.

"So why didn't you call me later?"

I thought quickly.

"I got too pissed, I didn't want to call you when I was like that. Sorry."

"Well, I hope you feel bad now then," she said, giving a scornful shake of her head.

"I do Shelley, honest. I'll make it up to you." I put my arms round her and went to kiss her but she turned away.

"Please Shelley, it won't happen again." Right then I needed her to be on my side. I went down on one knee and pleaded with her. "Please…" She looked at me, trying to be angry then she started laughing.

"Alright then, I forgive you. Your jeans are getting wet, stupid."

We went back to the flat and into my room. I lifted up her top. I felt the smooth skin on her stomach and the dip in the small of her back where her spine curved.

I tried to forget about the killing but even when I was inside her it was bothering me. I kept pushing it out of my mind hoping she wouldn't notice anything. Afterwards I fell into a deep sleep and she woke me up saying she had to get back. Things were going round and round in my head. I thought, hoped, that there wasn't anything to link us to the murder, hardly any CCTV and I didn't remember seeing anyone else in the park. On the Tube I'd kept my head down. I still needed an alibi though. I thought about my cousin, Alan, Ray's son. He owed me. When we were younger we hung out together – once he stole a car and burnt it out. He'd needed an alibi and I'd given him one. I hadn't seen him for years but I had to do something and it was the best idea I'd had. That was that decided and it was time to get rid of the scarf. I had the idea of feeding it down a drain a few streets away. The sewers could take it.

I put my hand in my jacket pocket expecting to touch silk but all I could feel was an old fag end. I checked the other side. It was empty. I tried the inside pocket, nothing. Shit. I started to panic, scouring the floor and under the bed but it wasn't there. I must have dropped it when I was talking to Chris, maybe when I pulled my fags out, which meant it must be lying around on the estate, anyone could find it. I took one more look round then went out, walking the same way I'd gone earlier, checking the pavements and gutters. The scarf was nowhere to be seen. I checked the route again but there was still no sign. Scared and frustrated I kicked the wall.

Back at the flat Mum was there. I hadn't seen her since it happened.

"Jimmy, I want you to tidy the living room, your stuff's all over it."

"I haven't got time. Liam can do it, half of it's his anyway."

"He does his share of the housework. It's time you did some."

She had that look on her face that she got when she'd been thinking about something for a while.

"I'll do it tomorrow."

"No Jimmy, I know what you're like, you'll go out and stay out and that will be that."

She was blocking the stairs. I tried to push past her but she stopped me. I knocked into her and she fell against the wall. She didn't make a sound but her face turned pale and she looked shocked. For a moment I wanted to stop and say sorry; instead I went into my room and shut the door.

12

VALERIE

On the third day I went with Renee to where it happened.

It was misty and cold. The common was wide, interspersed with paths and a stretch of water. We followed the path that led from north to south passing a playground and a cafe before reaching an area of trees and shrubs. Blue and white ribbons stretched across the grass tied to trees. I started walking in that direction; a bit of me wanted to be where it happened but Renee caught my arm.

"Let's stay here."

Renee kept hold and I leaned close to her, needing her certainty. I tried not to imagine his last minutes or hours. My eyes were drawn to a tree with low branches. There was one that had broken off and the newly exposed wood was orange-coloured and fleshy. Did that happen when he was trying to get away? Something rustled in the undergrowth and I spotted a blackbird rooting through dead leaves.

Several bunches of flowers were tied to a lamp post, others placed neatly on the ground. There were little notes attached. I'd brought a bunch of dark purple daisies that I set down on the grass. I shut my eyes and spoke a prayer.

As we stood there two young women wearing hijabs

approached. They were carrying a small bunch of flowers each. They seemed hesitant; one of them looked at me and gave a small smile. They put the flowers on the grass and stood with bent heads. Nobody spoke.

* * *

I couldn't make decisions, even simple things like what to wear or what to eat. Friends called to talk about Anton but none of them knew the truth about our relationship. The only person I wanted to see was Renee.

One day I went to the supermarket, the first time I'd been to a crowded place since the murder. I kept thinking people were looking at me. When I got to the till I fumbled for my purse and dropped it on the floor, I picked it up but when I took out my card couldn't remember my pin number.

The woman cashier said, "Are you alright, dear? You look a bit funny."

I thought she was suspicious of me but then I saw the concern on her face. Tears flowed down my cheeks and I tried to find a tissue.

"It's alright, take your time, you look like you've had a shock."

I managed to speak, "Sorry, I'll be alright in a minute."

Someone behind me sighed and the cashier said sharply, "We're going as fast as we can, thank you for being patient."

* * *

There was no word about when the funeral would be. I really wanted to talk to Anton's dad to see how he was and to tell him how important Anton was to me. I knew that his mum had died a few years ago and that his dad lived alone. One day we'd walked past the house and Anton had pointed it out, I remembered the white door with a red tulip in the glass above.

The house was in Honor Oak, one of several post-war houses built in the middle of a Victorian terrace, a reminder of bombs. I rang the bell and waited. The house looked closed up, the downstairs curtains were drawn even though it was the middle of the afternoon. I was about to turn away when I heard the sound of the lock.

The door opened about a foot and he peered around.

"Hello Mr Thomas, I'm Valerie, a friend of Anton's. We met once at the showcase, do you remember?"

He passed his hand across his eyes.

"Yes," he said slowly. "I remember."

"Sorry if I'm disturbing you. Can I talk to you for a minute?"

It seemed ages before he said, "Come in."

He walked down the hall ahead of me. I noticed that he had a slight limp and remembered Anton telling me about a hip operation. The living room was dark. He pulled the curtains apart and grey light filtered in. It was sparsely furnished; a maroon sofa, a table with two chairs and in the corner a small television. He stood by the table and didn't suggest that we sat down. I looked around, trying to imagine Anton as a child there, then turned to face him.

He bore a resemblance to Anton, his face was thinner and the hair mostly grey, but he had the same nose and mouth. His eyes were rimmed with red as if he'd been crying or maybe it was because he hadn't slept. Seeing him made it more real.

"I'm so sorry about Anton," I said, trying not to cry. He looked at me and away again, as if he couldn't bear to see anyone else's grief.

He picked up a framed photograph from the table and studied it as if he'd never seen it before.

"This is Anton when he was nine. Soon after it was taken he had a bicycle accident. It was before everyone started wearing helmets. He was unconscious for about an hour. The doctors thought he might have a brain injury. I remember Rose and me sitting at either side of his hospital bed. She was praying for him. He came back to us that time."

He shut his eyes for a moment as if hoping it would happen again. When he opened them he said, "I am glad Rose isn't alive to know this."

"It must be terrible to lose a child," I said.

He didn't answer and I wondered whether I'd said the wrong thing.

After another moment he said, "Anton said there was someone new, he didn't tell me much about his personal life so I thought it must mean something."

"We were friends at college, we only started going out a few weeks ago, after he split up with Leila."

He looked at me as if taking me in for the first time.

"He had everything to look forward to: acting, a family, a long time of happiness."

He sighed deeply and put the photo down.

I wondered whether I should ask about the investigation. As if he knew what I was thinking he said, "The police are keeping an open mind about the murder. They're looking at several theories, including that it might have been a racist attack. They have learned something perhaps."

I knew he was talking about Stephen Lawrence and the huge fight that his parents had to get his murder properly investigated. It had happened when I was four. I heard about it from my mum and dad and I took in that a young man was killed for no other reason than he looked like me. His name became as familiar as if he'd been part of my own family.

"There is a liaison officer who's keeping me informed. She said as soon as there's more information she'll let me know."

I wanted the person caught but I didn't think I could bear to see their face, know that that human being was capable of such cruelty.

We were silent for a moment then I said, "He was a wonderful actor. He made you feel things."

He nodded. "Rose encouraged him to sing from when he was little. She knew songs from many musicals. He soon picked them up and started singing them on his own. I didn't think it was a good idea at first; I was worried about money and him not being able to support a family. David was never interested in art, he liked to analyse things instead, he used to turn his toys upside down and shake them until all the insides fell out. I am frightened about his future now."

He looked even more fragile and put his hand on the back of the chair in order to steady himself. I would have liked to have given him a hug and told him it would be alright but I didn't know if it would.

"Is there anything I can do to help?" I said. I wanted to stay longer, just to listen to his voice, which had the same tone as Anton's, with the sound of the Caribbean. It was the first time I'd felt anything other than very lonely since I'd heard the news. If things had been different, I would have become a part of this family.

"Thank you but David is coming tomorrow to help me. Please come to the funeral."

The thought of it was terrible but I said yes.

* * *

When I came out of the house it was almost dark. Overhead the clouds were huge, black and moving fast. A gust of wind hit me, nearly pushing me into the road. I was passing a row of shops when a young woman came out of a bar. Her coat caught my eye, black with white polka dots, tightly belted. She turned to wave at someone, then walked to the bus stop and stood in the shelter in front of an illuminated panel. A gust of wind caught her scarf and it lifted and billowed out. I noticed the colours and stopped – breath catching in my throat.

She was looking at her phone and didn't notice me staring. I moved closer. The scarf was just like the one I'd given Anton, pink and orange with the same swirling pattern. I couldn't believe she had one too. When I bought it they told me that every scarf the artist made was unique.

I had an urge to reach forward and touch it, see if it was silk, but just then a bus drew up, people surged towards the door and she disappeared amongst them. Hesitating, I wondered whether to follow. After a moment she appeared on the top deck near the front. I tried to catch her eye but she was looking straight ahead. The bus started to pull away. I watched it go, trying to make sense of what I'd seen.

Since the murder I'd noticed I couldn't always trust my

mind. Twice I thought I'd seen Anton; once in a crowded shop and then on the other side of the street but when I'd looked again they were nothing like him. I could have been wrong about the scarf. The light at the bus stop had a yellowish tinge and might have altered the colours.

It started to rain hard. I began to walk, the wind pushing me forwards. Brake lights were reflected in the wet pavement. Glowing red spots interspersed with wide circles of the streetlamps. When I got home I took off my jacket, turned on the heating and pulled a chair close to the radiator, waiting for it to warm up. Most of the heat went straight into the roof. It was too hot in summer and too cold in winter.

I thought about the girl. She looked a bit younger than me. She was white, with long black hair, small and slim. Perhaps she too had gone to the shop in Oxford. Or perhaps she had a boyfriend who saw the scarf and thought it would go well with her polka-dot coat. The shop assistant could have been wrong about it being a one-off. Perhaps I was going mad. I'd heard that grief could make you like that.

I wanted to tell someone. I thought about Matthew but didn't think he'd understand the significance of it so I called Renee.

"Are you OK?" she said.

"I think I saw someone wearing Anton's scarf."

"What scarf?"

"I gave him one as a present, it was really beautiful. I saw a woman wearing it."

"She must have bought one the same."

"It was a one-off."

"They might have said that in the shop to make you buy it."

I didn't answer and after a few seconds she said, "I know it's really hard dealing with this Valerie. I miss Anton too but it must be much worse for you."

"I'm not imagining it, Renee."

There was a pause then she said, "Who was it?"

I told her about what I'd seen.

"I wish I'd followed her now but I was so shocked I couldn't think. Anton told me he loved the scarf and wore it all the time, now he's been killed."

"Oh no. That's horrible then. How come she had it?"

"That's what I want to know," I said.

13

JIMMY

I'd heard about mothers shopping their sons so I needed to keep Mum sweet. I told her I was sorry for pushing her but that I had a lot on my mind then I cleaned the living room and did all the washing-up.

Chris and me met up again and agreed on a text code to say whether there were cops sniffing about. 'Millwall' meant all clear, 'Watford' meant danger.

The next thing to do was get in touch with Alan about an alibi but before I could do that Shelley called. She said she had something to show me and to meet her in a bar later. I asked what was going on but she said it was a surprise. When I got there I ordered a lager for myself and a white wine for her. I was halfway down the bottle when I saw her coming through the door. She looked gorgeous. A few blokes turned to stare as she walked past. She came up to kiss me but I was focussed on what she had on round her neck. She saw my expression and stopped still.

"What's wrong?"

"Where did you get that?" I hissed, eyes on the scarf.

She put her hand up to touch it.

"This? I found it in your pocket. Nice, isn't it?"

She was acting nonchalant.

"What were you doing going through my pockets?"

"Looking for your cigarettes."

"You don't smoke."

"I thought I might start," she said, casually, pulling out the chair and sitting opposite.

"Take it off," I said, keeping my voice low. I didn't want anyone starting to pay attention.

"Why? Does it belong to your other girlfriend, the one you've been spending so much time with?"

"That's stupid, Shelley, I haven't got anyone else." If only it was as simple as that.

"Don't call me that." Her face changed from innocent to angry. "This is a woman's scarf, how come you've got it?"

I needed her to take it off.

"If you must know I got it for you then I changed my mind. I didn't think it would suit you. I was right, it doesn't."

She looked at me suspiciously.

"Is that the truth?"

"Yes. It doesn't belong to another woman." That much at least was true.

"The thing is, I don't believe you Jimmy. It doesn't look new, someone's worn it. And anyway you've changed recently. You used to pay me loads of attention, now you just want to go drinking. You say you're with your mates but how do I know you're telling me the truth?"

Her voice was getting louder and people were turning to look.

"Give me the scarf, Shelley."

It must have sounded worse than what I meant. She pushed her chair back and stood up.

"If you threaten me I'm going," she said.

I caught her arm. "We can sort this out, it's not what you think."

She wrenched her arm away. "Piss off Jimmy."

At the next table a man stood up, looking like he was about to come over.

She started heading for the door.

"Fuck," I muttered. I grabbed my jacket and followed her. The man sat back down again as if relieved he didn't have to do anything.

She was walking fast up the road. I ran after her.

"Leave me alone," she said and began walking even quicker. I caught her arm and pushed her against a wall. I grabbed the end of the scarf. She tried to stop me but I unwound it with one quick movement and whipped it away.

She screamed, "I hate you Jimmy," and started crying. It had gone too far for me to feel sorry for her.

"You shouldn't have done that, Shelley."

Shoving the scarf in my pocket I walked away, cursing because I knew I'd been a fucking idiot. I should have got rid of it straight away. Now she knew about it. She didn't understand what it was and I couldn't tell her. It was a mess and a dangerous one.

I headed to the industrial estate in Rotherhithe, passing the skip lorries waiting to dump their waste and turned into a street of old warehouses which were waiting to be pulled down. They'd been waiting for years. No one lived round there. Most of the buildings were boarded up but I knew my way into one of them. Despite the gaps in the roof some parts of the concrete floor were dry. I pulled the scarf out and dropped it on the ground, got out my lighter, squatted down and held the flame at the edge. It took a few seconds to catch. The fabric seemed to melt and then dissolve as the flames edged along it. Suddenly it flared up, the ends curled and disintegrated. Standing up I kicked away the pile of grey black ash.

There was a sound on the corrugated roof like falling stones. I watched through the gap as the rain came down. Every now and then a gust of wind blew water inside. I backed further in and lit a fag, waiting for it to stop. After a while I realised I was starving and starting to freeze so I headed out into the rain.

14

VALERIE

The news said that the police were questioning a suspect. For hours I kept checking the website to see if they'd charged anyone but there was no more news. I wished I could talk to someone who knew more than me but I didn't want to bother Mr Thomas. Next day the police let the person go.

I was back working at the cafe. I was lucky that they kept my job open for me but I missed being at the theatre, with the other actors, suspended in a make-believe world. The real world seemed bleak, with no future.

The picture of the woman at the bus stop kept returning to my mind. I could see the polka-dot coat and the scarf blowing in the wind. What if my intuition was right and she was connected to the murder? I wished I'd grabbed the opportunity and followed, it was probably the only chance I'd get to talk to her. I thought about going to the police but they'd probably see me as just another grieving person clutching at straws – they might be kind but they'd send me away as soon as they could.

For nights on end I tossed and turned, trying to figure out what to do, then at last I decided to go and look for the scarf and the girl. Not because I thought I'd find her, but I knew that doing nothing was driving me crazy.

When I saw her she'd been coming out of a wine bar at about 6 p.m. If that was where she worked she might always use the same bus stop so I decided to start there. After work I made my way to Dulwich and stood in the shelter. I waited for what seemed like ages. People came and went. I looked at the advert for so long I could have drawn the model's face in precise detail. She didn't come.

Maybe she only worked there on a Friday, which was when I'd seen her. On the Friday afterwards I swopped my shift at work so I could arrive earlier. There were around fifteen people waiting but she wasn't one of them. Four buses pulled up at the same time and when they moved off I was the only person left. I was about to give up when I saw her, heading towards me, spotted coat swinging out. I watched, not taking my eyes off her.

As she got closer I saw her coat was open at the neck and, with a shock, that her throat was white and exposed. I thought she might not appear, but not that she'd be without the scarf. I didn't know what to do. It seemed weird to ask about something she wasn't wearing but if I didn't I knew I'd be left wondering again and probably still think I was losing my mind.

I went over to where she was standing. "Hi, can I ask you something?"

She looked up from her mobile, surprised.

"What?"

"I noticed you here last week and you were wearing a really nice scarf."

The effect was dramatic. Her mouth dropped open, she turned red then pale. She put her hand up to her neck.

"What are you talking about?" she said in a faint voice.

I knew I was on to something.

"I was admiring it, that's all, I wondered where you bought it."

"Who are you?" she said, backing away.

"My name's Valerie."

She turned away and I thought she was going to refuse to speak to me but she swung round and said, "Do you know Jimmy?"

I shook my head. "No, why?"

"We had a fight. He took the scarf," she said.

"Why did he do that?"

I knew as soon as I said it I sounded too eager.

"I don't know you. You can't start interrogating strangers, it's out of order."

"My boyfriend was wearing a scarf like that when he was killed."

She stared at me as if she thought I was mad.

I carried on talking, trying to explain. "I gave it to him. It was a designer scarf, a one-off."

"You're talking about crazy stuff. It's nothing to do with me."

She looked behind her. We both saw the bus coming. She pulled her coat tighter. I couldn't stop her from going. As she was getting on I called out, "Think about it, please."

She drew her shoulders closer together so I knew she'd heard.

* * *

After she'd gone I sat in the bus shelter. I felt bruised by the encounter, her hostility, though I knew I'd probably shocked her with what I'd said. I tried to figure out what it all meant. Even if the scarf was different there was something strange going on otherwise why would she have fought with her boyfriend over it? It went round and round in my head but I couldn't figure out an innocent explanation for her reaction.

Before I could be sure there was a connection I needed to make certain that there really was only one scarf like that, so I went back to Oxford. It was the same bus journey I'd done three weeks ago. This time the green fields looked mournful and neglected. I leaned my head against the window and thought about Anton's touch on my back.

Despite the cold the city was busy with tourists. I stood outside the shop looking at the window display. This time it was of shoes and bags, primary colours, red with a flash of blue, yellow with a diagonal stripe of purple. I went inside. The assistant was the same one as before. She looked up and smiled.

"Can I help you?"

I wanted to say, 'I bought a scarf from you and now the person I gave it to is dead,' but it was too shocking.

"I bought a really beautiful scarf here a while ago. It was orange and pink with wavy lines. I… I left it on a train. I wanted to know if you had another one the same?"

"I remember you now and I know the one you mean. It was lovely. The artist only made one of each design. There was the one you bought, one with turquoise and lilac spirals and one with yellow triangles on green. We sold them all in the space of a week. We asked her to make some more but she said that wasn't how she worked."

"Oh. It's just that I thought I saw a girl wearing the same scarf and I wondered if there were several."

"Definitely not. Maybe she found it on the train?"

So it was the only one, which meant I might have met someone who knew Anton's murderer. For a moment I felt like I was floating out of my body. I stood staring out of the window.

"Are you alright?" she said.

"It's just strange that I saw it again."

When I got home I lay on the bed with my coat on, staring at the ceiling, trying to think. I'd been given a sign but because the girl refused to talk to me I couldn't do anything about it. I had something and nothing, a scarf blowing in the wind, a scarf I'd probably never see again. Like Anton. I put my headphones on and listened to Salif Keita. His voice had lifted me out of some terrible places but today it was as if my body was in a shell, preventing the music from reaching me.

I was so shattered. Grief coloured everything. My sense of myself seemed shaky, like water on a mirror obscuring my reflection. Nothing made sense. My dreams of becoming a great Shakespearean actor were over. I must separate myself from them. I would strip away my desire like a snake slipping out of its skin. Becoming an actor had given me purpose and a sense of hope about my life. Whenever I'd doubted my acting ability I was spurred on by Anton. We were on that path together, how could I carry on without him?

The narrow bookshelf fitting the space by the side of the door before the ceiling started to slope down was full of plays, grouped together under playwrights, alphabetically. I still had the copy of *A Midsummer Night's Dream* that Dad had given me. I took it down and looked at it. It was battered on the spine and there were marks on the cover. I wished he were there.

On the next shelf were studies of texts and related biographies. I started taking them off the shelves, thinking at first I might clean them and put them back, but instead began making a pile on the table. With each book it was like another piece of the dream breaking away but I couldn't stop. When I'd finished I took the books over to the window and blew the dust off. The new tower block being built on the other side of the park was rising. My view was constricting.

I cleaned the shelves. I could put my small sculptures there; they would look good. The piles of books went into carrier bags.

15

JIMMY

Every time the doorbell rang I jumped. I didn't want Mum or Liam getting suspicious so I was keeping out of the house as much as possible. I wasn't eating much. I'd never been overweight but now my jeans were falling off me. Luckily Mum was too busy to notice.

The day after Shelley and me argued, I asked Ray about Alan.

"I'd like to catch up with him. We used to be good mates."

Ray was painting window frames. He looked round.

"Haven't seen him in months, he fell out with Mandy. He was hanging out with a girl she didn't like, a Goth or something, all black fingernails and huge boots. I thought she was alright myself but you know Mandy, a bit intolerant."

I couldn't imagine Alan going out with someone like that.

"You don't know where he is then?" I said, trying not to sound desperate.

"I've got a number but it may be out of date, I haven't tried it recently. If you speak to him say I'd like to see him."

The phone rang for ages then went to answerphone,

which wasn't Alan's voice. I didn't leave a message. I tried again later and got the answerphone but this time I left a message and he got straight back to me.

"What's up Jimmy? Haven't heard from you for a while."

"Wanted to catch up that's all. I'm working with your dad now."

"I feel sorry for you. I've got no time for him, he never stood up to Mum about Evie."

"There's something I want to ask you."

"What's that then?"

"Not on the phone, can I come round?"

"Sure, you can meet Evie too."

He gave me his address, which was in Catford. When I arrived at the house he was out the front under the bonnet of an old car. I said "Hi" and he poked his head out. His hands were covered in oil. He wiped one on a piece of rag and stuck it out.

"Alright mate, good to see you," he said.

We went inside. The back door was open and the yard was full of twisted bits of metal. I poked my head out and saw things that looked like totem poles. When I looked closer I could make out pieces of engine that had been welded together.

"That's Evie's stuff, she's a sculptor, makes things out of the parts I can't use, recycling she calls it." He sounded proud. "She'll be back soon."

I wondered what sort of girl he'd hooked up with.

"What did you want to ask me?"

I hadn't decided exactly what to say. The story had to be believable.

"I need an alibi."

"What you been up to, committing murder?"

Like he knew. I laughed, trying to make it convincing. "Nothing like that. Someone I was with was in a fight. Turned out the bloke got a serious injury so I need to place myself somewhere else."

He folded his arms and looked at me. "Who was this geezer, the one you beat up?"

"Not me, someone else."

"If I'm going to lie for you I like to know what I'm doing it for."

Just then the front door opened and a voice called, "Hello."

"Come and meet Jimmy, we're in the kitchen."

She was really tall and skinny. Her boots had platform soles about six inches thick; without them she probably would have been normal height. Her hair was long and black, dyed, not natural like Shelley's and she had black eye make-up on.

"Hello Jimmy, nice to meet you."

I was surprised because when she smiled she looked quite pretty.

She looked from me to Alan. "No resemblance then. I've heard about your misspent youth. What are you up to now?"

"Oh you know, this and that."

I didn't want to get into conversation with her because I needed to sort stuff out with Alan.

"We're going down the pub sweetheart, you can come if you like."

"No it's OK, I'll let you two catch up. I've got some work to do."

She went out into the yard, put on a pair of goggles and picked up the welding tool.

Now I'd seen her I didn't want to tell Alan that the geezer was black. Evie wasn't but she was weird, different.

After I'd got the drinks in I raised the subject again, told him the date and half of what'd happened, except that the guy got beaten up, not that he died.

"What was that date again? 7th February?"

"That was it, happened in Rotherhithe so I need to be somewhere else, where there's no CCTV so they can't verify it."

"Wasn't that when that bloke got done over on the common, the black geezer?"

Somehow it must have stuck in his mind.

"Was it? I don't remember." I was turning the beer mat over and over.

He put down his pint and stared at me across the table with clear pale-blue eyes. He did that a lot when we were younger.

"You weren't mixed up in that were you? If you were I can't help you. I can't stand racism, makes my stomach churn."

"I swear it wasn't that, we were miles away from there and the geezer was white."

He kept looking at me and I could see he was thinking hard. I was praying he was going to say yes, there was no one else to ask, but he said, "Sorry mate, I can't do it. After the last time I got nicked I swore to Evie I'd go straight and I don't want to get caught for giving a false alibi. You'll have to ask someone else."

I could tell he'd made up his mind.

Shit.

* * *

I was in my room listening to music and didn't hear Liam until he practically yelled in my ear.

"Been out with Shelley?"

"What's it to you?" I grunted.

"Just wondering."

"What?"

"Whether you've got a bit on the side."

I pulled off the headphones. "Leave it out. You know me better than that."

"I bumped into her yesterday." He was leaning against the wall, arms folded like he had an agenda.

"And?"

"She said you had a row."

"Just a minor misunderstanding that's all." I shrugged.

"She said you hurt her."

"Bollocks. You know me better than that. I'd never hit a woman."

"Hurt her," he said, persistent.

"It's none of your business but if you must know she nicked something of mine, I got it back off her that's all. She took it the wrong way and went running off. She gets wound up about stuff, you know what girls are like."

"Shelley's straight, you said that yourself. What did she take?"

"A watch Granddad gave me. It was broken, I was thinking of getting it mended."

I avoided his eyes. Liam knew me well enough to know if I was lying.

"You involved with something dodgy?"

"What do you mean?"

"You've been acting strange recently."

"Got a few things on my mind that's all."

He gave me a look and said, "You should sort it out else you'll lose her."

He went out shutting the door hard. I cursed Shelley for talking to him.

* * *

There was no one else I could ask to be an alibi. I had no money to offer as a bribe. I thought about Liam but he already thought something was up; besides, he seemed to be getting more and more moral, like he'd got religion or something.

Though I was still angry with Shelley I missed her, having a laugh, making out, her hair draped all over my chest. I called her but she didn't answer. After a few days she texted and said she wanted to meet up.

She turned up looking sexy as hell. I wanted her straight away but her expression was a turn off.

"We need to talk."

"Look Shelley, I was in a really bad temper that day, let's forget it."

She shook her head. "It's not only that. Something else happened. I met this mad woman outside work. She asked me about the scarf, the one you tore off me. She said all this stuff about her boyfriend. Told me he was murdered and he was wearing a scarf like that when it happened."

I couldn't believe what I was hearing.

"For fuck's sake Shelley, who was she?"

"Don't swear at me. I don't know who she was, I never saw her before. She was black, not old."

She was standing with her arms folded and still hadn't taken off her coat.

Her expression annoyed me and I grasped her arm, a bit harder than I meant to. "What did you say to her?"

"That hurts." She pulled her arm away. "Nothing. It was scary, I'm telling you. I got away from her. Where did you get that scarf? I want to know the truth."

"I can't remember the shop's name, it was in the West End, one of those ones that sells jewellery and stuff."

She looked at me and I could see she was trying to work out whether I was telling the truth or not. I had my best innocent face on.

"So she's lying then?"

"Yeah Shelley. You said yourself she was mad."

She sat on the bed. I could tell I was winning the argument.

"You promise it's got nothing to do with you?"

"I promise. Now come here, I've missed you, I'm sorry about the fight but it's over. Can we talk about something else?"

She looked dubious but I pulled her close and told her that I loved her. I unbuttoned her coat and lifted up her yellow jumper. I began to stroke her breasts. She was kissing me. I was turned on but trouble was now I knew about this woman. There was no way it was just a coincidence or that she was crazy; there had to be more to it than that especially as she was black. It could have been her boyfriend that Chris killed and now there was evidence pointing to me.

Shelley undid my jeans and for a while everything else went out of my mind.

16

VALERIE

Before they could release Anton's body there needed to be a post-mortem, which seemed to be taking forever. I wanted to be at the funeral with everyone to say a proper goodbye. I felt as if I was holding my breath underwater and soon my lungs would burst. Days went past and there was still no news then finally the date was set – 3rd March, 10.30 a.m., South London Crematorium.

I woke early, my stomach clenched as it always did whenever I was nervous. It seemed strange to be frightened of an event that was just very sad. I wasn't sure what to wear and laid several things out on the bed. Although Anton loved bright colours I didn't want to offend anyone so finally I chose a black skirt and a black jacket. Underneath the jacket I wore a purple shirt and my tiger print belt that Anton liked. He said it was like a cat wrapped round my waist. As I fastened the silver clasp I kept my hands there, trying to imagine his fingers on mine.

The last funeral I'd been at was Dad's, twelve years ago. I remembered the table with the food and beer and Mum trying to get me to eat a sandwich but all I wanted was for him to come home.

I met Renee at the entrance and we walked through the cemetery towards the crematorium, which was set within a circle of trees. Low cloud hovered over the tops. It was as cold as ever. As we got closer I saw Mr Thomas standing by the door and next to him a tall young man, who I knew must be David, though he didn't look like Anton. More and more people were arriving. Anton had a lot of friends, both black and white, and I remembered him telling me he had eight cousins.

Renee and I stood to the side waiting. I was shivering with cold.

"Are you OK, Valerie?"

I nodded unable to speak.

We were there for a while then the hearse appeared at the gates. There was to be no resurrection. As it passed I made myself look at the coffin. I took in the polished wood, the brass handles and the bunch of white lilies on top before averting my eyes. The undertakers carried it into the building and we followed, taking a seat a few rows from the front. I caught sight of Matthew sitting on the opposite side of the room. He looked over and gave a brief smile.

When everyone was seated the vicar began to talk about Anton's life. I could tell he was trying to be sincere but his words could have been about anyone. After he finished we sang a hymn that I didn't recognise. I was waiting to feel something other than frozen.

David stood up. He began reading from a piece of paper. His voice was like Anton's; he had the same rhythm of speech and the same deep voice. After a minute he put the notes down and looked at us.

"My brother…" his voice broke up. He looked down at

his hands and then began again. "My brother was different to me. He was an artist; he wanted to make people think. He was good at reaching out, making connections with people, that's why so many of us are here. He was capable of great passion, something that's a gift and that we will all miss."

Listening to him articulate what I'd lost released something and I began to cry.

"He didn't deserve to die. He didn't deserve to be killed in a random robbery or targeted by racists." There were loud murmurs of agreement. "We must fight to find out who killed him but most of all we must mourn his loss and make a promise to him to live good lives. That's what he'd have wanted."

He finished speaking and stood at the front with his head bowed. There was a period of quiet. Some people were crying, others were praying. I saw their mouths moving, their hands locked together. I thought about the first time we kissed and about the delight on his face the next morning. I tried to cry quietly but some of the sobs broke loose. Renee put her arm around me.

As the curtains began to close around the coffin they played the last piece of music, Marvin Gaye's 'What's Going On'. It was crushingly appropriate.

* * *

Renee said she had to get back to work. She kissed me goodbye and said, "Be strong."

Mr Thomas was the last person to come out of the building as if he didn't want to say goodbye. He saw me and came over.

"You are coming to the house?"

"Yes."

The living room was crammed with people. I said hello to several of Anton's friends. Matthew wasn't there. Maybe he thought he wouldn't be welcome because the thing he was involved in might be the reason Anton was killed.

I wanted to talk to David but held back, thinking I wasn't proper family, then I noticed he was standing on his own so I went over.

"I'm Valerie. Thank you for the speech, it was wonderful."

He looked at me. "Are you one of his actor friends?"

I nodded.

"Were you his girlfriend?"

It was hard to speak without crying. "We'd just started…"

"Shit," he said, loudly.

People turned to look and his dad said, "David."

"Sorry. I can't stand around being quiet and reasonable. I'm going outside."

He headed for the door. I followed; it didn't seem right that he went on his own.

He was leaning against the wall, his head back. He looked as if he wanted to bang it against the brick.

Despair encircled us like a cloud of vapour.

"I hate the way we all just accept what's happened. I've got a kid on the way in Manchester otherwise I'd come down and find the bastards that did this."

Anger vibrated through him.

"Do you think they'll make an arrest soon?"

He looked at me as if I was crazy. "There was no CCTV. Only one person's come forward. He said he thought he saw a small group of people in a corner of the park but he didn't take much notice of them. They haven't found a weapon. I want to be able to trust the police to do their job but things haven't changed much. I still get stopped and searched. The last time there were four of them, all over me. I asked them what it was about and they said, 'Reasonable grounds, mate, reasonable grounds.' They didn't find anything of course."

I had to tell him the truth, even if it made him hate me.

"He'd come to London partly because of me. If we hadn't started seeing each other he might still be alive."

"No way this is your fault," he said, with such fierceness that I jumped. "You're innocent, as was Anton. Black people get made to feel that things are their fault."

I thought about that and realised I'd been blaming myself since the night it'd happened.

He moved away from the wall and said, "I better get back and make sure Dad's OK. He's holding it together but he's destroyed."

"I have to go now," I said. "Can you tell him I said goodbye?"

"Sure but please go to see him again, I can tell he likes you."

I went home, got undressed and crawled into bed. I curled up on my side and pulled the duvet over me.

17

JIMMY

I was having nightmares every night. Vivid pictures of swaying trees, branches like fingers. Sometimes it was pitch black and I could hear feet pounding on the path, someone breathing in short bursts, a scream and a long, low groan. When I woke up my body felt as if it'd been pummelled in a boxing ring.

I bumped into Chris as I was heading out of the estate to work. He stopped to talk which I was surprised about, said we were going to get away with it, asked me to go to football with him that Saturday. He didn't know about Shelley and the scarf, he might not be so sure then. I was hoping that the mad woman was just that and she knew nothing about the murder.

We were playing Leicester at home. They were already in the play-offs. It was going to be a dogfight. We had a couple of pints in the Dog and Ball, then joined the other fans walking to the match, draped in blue and white, telling jokes, catching up with news. The path ran alongside the railway tracks, through a procession of arches, kids stopping to jump on the cripple tree, an old oak with one branch hanging down, almost touching the ground, like me and Wayne used to do when we went with Dad.

Chris had a season ticket and the seats weren't bad, halfway down the Cold Blow Lane end, in front of Roy, the nutter, who shouted even when nothing was happening, "Oi Pearson, you fucking gargoyle, who let you out then?"

The first half was crap, we were useless and they were even worse. It was looking like it was going to be a nil-nil draw, but Kenny must've said something to the boys at half-time because they came out looking lively. They started chasing down the ball and stringing half decent crosses together. We were singing, '*No one likes us, we don't care.*' Quick as a flash Keogh raced down the left wing, crossed the ball into the box and Taylor was there, flicking it neatly onto his right foot and straight into the net. The stadium rose, arms in the air, cheering. The Leicester fans stayed sitting and silent.

The rest of the game was scrappy but Shittu kept everything at bay. We ended up a point behind Leicester, next in line for the play-off places. Not a bad result.

Chris was full of it on the way home, talking about our chances of getting promotion. Three weeks ago he'd stuck a knife in someone, now he was getting on with life as if it had never happened.

I said, "I asked my cousin about an alibi but he said no."

He flashed me a look. "Get onto it, you never know when they might be round asking questions. Talk to Tyler."

"What's he got to do with it?"

Shrugging he said, "He knows what happened. He sussed it out from the timing, asked me straight out and I didn't disagree with him. He said, 'That's one less on the street' and he hoped the person who did it gets away with it."

I respected Tyler and believed what he had to say about our country but I didn't know if I trusted him. He could be like everyone else in power. Acting like they're on your side but next minute they're shopping their granny to get what they want.

"What if he drops us in it?" I wanted to say 'you' but I knew he was going to make me take half the blame.

He laughed and shrugged. "They don't want their names dragged through the mud. They would if there was a trial."

* * *

The more I thought about it the more I realised Chris was right – Tyler was my only hope. I went to his lettings office to talk to him. He looked up from the desk as I came in.

"OK Jimmy, what can I do for you?"

"I need to ask a favour," I said, feeling like a kid trying to get something off my dad. He always said no.

"What do you need?"

"An alibi for 7th February," I said, straight out because I knew he didn't like bullshit.

"I understand there was some sort of altercation that night."

"That's right."

"You need to be placed somewhere else?"

"Yes."

He smiled and nodded, as if he'd known all along what I was going to ask. "It will come at a price, Jimmy." Leaning back in his chair he surveyed me. I shifted from one foot to the other wondering what he was going to ask me to do. I knew I had to agree to it, whatever it was. "As it happens I might have a job for you. You know that our brothers and sisters are coming over from Scandinavia. Communications will have to happen when they get here. We need someone who doesn't draw attention to themselves – someone who moves quietly. Think you can do that?"

"You won't even notice me," I said.

"Right, well I hope I can trust you, Jimmy."

"I promise I'll keep my mouth shut." This was easy. If it was all I had to do I'd got off lightly.

"I'll let you know what's needed nearer the time. I've got someone in mind for your alibi."

I thanked him, ran down the three flights of stairs and pushed open the door to the street. The sun was out for the first time in weeks. Tyler would defend me. That was the best news I'd had for a while.

18

VALERIE

My shift patterns were long which was good because they stopped me from thinking. The problem was the minute I got back home it all started again, round and round, the scarf, the girl, like a film stuck on a loop. I thought about David, his anger and what he'd said about finding out who did it. It seemed as if my grief had overwhelmed my desire to act. The police still hadn't charged anyone. Maybe the scarf was real evidence and I was doing nothing about it. I decided to call Matthew, find out if he could help.

"I'm in the middle of a mailout, why don't you come over? I could do with the company."

"How are you?" he said, when I arrived.

"I'm OK," I lied.

"I just need to finish this pile. Have a seat."

He gestured to an armchair, which had a patch of stuffing coming out of the side like a lesion on the skin. I watched as he put magazines into brown envelopes and stuck address labels on them.

"Have the police told you anything?" I said.

"Nothing. You could ask his dad, they're meant to keep the family informed."

I shook my head. "I don't want to keep bothering him."

"No, I understand."

"The thing is – I saw someone wearing Anton's scarf."

He looked at me over the pile of magazines. "What scarf?"

"The one I gave him as a present. He said he'd wear it when I next saw him; that was the night he died. I talked to the girl wearing it and she said she'd argued with her boyfriend, Jimmy, about it."

He stopped what he was doing.

"You better explain."

I told him about the conversation at the bus stop, thinking he was going to laugh but he looked serious.

"The scarf might be a different one but it's interesting they had an argument."

"It was definitely the same. I even went back to the shop and they told me there was only ever one with that pattern. Do you think I should tell the police?"

"No I don't," he said. "Sorry, I don't think you'll convince them it's worth looking into, it's just a scarf after all."

He started sticking on labels again. I looked at him, thinking I shouldn't have trusted him.

"I've got to go now." I stood up and started putting on my coat.

"Hang on a minute, Valerie." He stood up too. "I don't mean forget about it all together. It could be significant; it's just that the police might not think so. Stay a bit longer."

He looked worried that he'd offended me. I hovered for a minute then sat down again. He pushed the magazines to one side and faced me. "Let's think about it logically.

We know the scarf was a one-off. We know that Anton was going to meet you when he was attacked and he was wearing the scarf, then somehow this girl got it. What I don't understand is, if it's linked to the murder, why didn't – Jimmy, was it – get rid of it?"

He was right. It didn't make sense. I felt deflated. Maybe I was just imagining the connection between them because I wanted it to be true.

"I've heard of people keeping things, like trophies, from the victims, or maybe he's just stupid and didn't see its significance," I said.

"If he's a racist it could be that. They're idiots, those people, dangerous and stupid, being stupid makes you dangerous. There's not much to go on but I'll ask around, see if anyone knows someone called Jimmy."

"Thanks."

I didn't think it would come to anything but it was something to occupy my mind which, having been so full of plans and hope, was now purposeless.

* * *

The days after the funeral seemed worse. Although it was traumatic before it there was something to aim for, now there was just bleak reality and the fact that Anton was no longer in my life.

I was sitting eating supper alone one night when Matthew called. "I've found something out, can you come over?"

I pushed my plate aside, got up and pulled on my coat. I was at his flat in half an hour. The laptop was open on the table.

"Jake phoned. He's just got back from South America."

"Who's Jake?"

"A member of our organisation who's been monitoring the activities of the NER. He heard about Anton's murder while he was away. After he got back and checked his other email account he found one from Anton dated the 7th February."

My heart felt as if it'd missed a few beats. It was the day he died.

"What did it say?"

He clicked a button on the laptop and a fuzzy picture appeared on the screen. Two men were standing outside what looked like an office building. I peered at it trying to make them out. One of the faces was in profile and all I could see was that he had dark hair. The other man was turning towards the camera, his features were blurred but I could see that he had short hair and a thin face and looked quite young.

"What was his message?" There had to be something, some words to go with the image but Matthew shook his head.

"Nothing, sorry."

I wanted him to have left something personal, just for me, but of course he didn't know then he was going to be killed.

He must have noticed my expression.

"I don't know why he sent it to Jake, he probably knew he had to hurry, perhaps it was the first address that came up."

"It's marked 8.15 p.m. The police said Anton was killed about 9.30 p.m.," I said.

We looked at each other, trying to take in what it meant.

"It has to be significant," he said.

"One of them could be Jimmy. I wonder where it was taken." I looked at the photo again. The building didn't have anything to distinguish it.

"Maybe Anton thought he was onto something. Jake was doing research into a far right Scandinavian group. We heard rumours that they might be coming over but no one knows for certain. These two could be significant."

I could feel fear creeping into my body. "I had no idea he was doing anything like that," I said.

"The plan was to keep everything quiet until we knew more. He was leaving Sheffield wasn't he? He said he wanted to be more involved."

I supposed there were many things I didn't know about Anton's life. We'd only just become really close. Before that all we ever talked about was acting.

"The police probably have ways of working out who they are. Even with the blurring, they can do face recognition and that stuff," I said.

"Yeah, we could go to the police," he sounded doubtful. "The problem is if those two know the cops are after them they'll probably clam up. Defend each other. I think we should find out who they are first," he said.

"How? We don't even know where the photo was taken."

Matthew's mobile rang. "Hi Jake. She's here." There was a silence while he listened to the voice on the other end. "Right, that's interesting. Thanks."

"One of our members who's doing undercover work says she knows who the one on the left is; she recognises

the V-shape hairline, you can just make it out if you look."
He flicked the photo open again and I looked closely.

"That's Chris Mayhew. She said he's more of a street fighter than political but he could have changed. Maybe they want to attract more thugs into the organisation."

"Does she know who the other one is?"

"She didn't recognise him. We need to get more information, get closer to the NER, maybe infiltrate one of their meetings."

"What can I do?"

He looked at me. "You're too…"

"What, too black?"

He looked embarrassed. "Too visible. It's dangerous. I don't want you to become a target too. I'll ask Jake and the others later."

"Maybe we could try talking to that girl again. She's scared but if we catch her off guard she might tell us more about Jimmy."

He nodded. "Have you got any ideas how to find her?"

"I think she works in a bar in Dulwich. When I first saw her she was coming out of there; she looked like she was leaving work. I don't even know her name. When I told her about Anton she was shocked but as if it made sense too, if you see what I mean."

"You're right, we need to find her."

The doorbell rang and he went to answer it. He came back, followed by a tall man with grey hair.

"This is Leonard. He's dropping off a copy of his latest book. He was head of the AF for a long time before deciding to write. This is Valerie."

"Nice to meet you," he said, smiling and shaking my hand.

"Maybe you could tell him about Anton sometime?" Matthew said.

I didn't want to talk about what happened to Anton as if he was some sort of statistic or campaign. I shook my head. "I've got to go now."

19

JIMMY

Now I'd got my alibi sorted I was less jumpy. If the cops came sniffing round I could prove I was somewhere else. Without any CCTV or forensics they had nothing. Chris had got rid of the phone and knife. He never told me where, just that no one would ever find them. Chris and me didn't see that much of each other. It was like he didn't want me around reminding him of what he'd done, but Shelley and me were good again. She was busy doing her new course and had forgotten about the scarf.

The NER was preparing to meet the group from Scandinavia. Only the main representatives were coming, but altogether with our members we were expecting at least two hundred. Tyler gave me a lot of work taking messages. He didn't trust electronic communication; there was surveillance everywhere, even on pay-as-you-go phones. I delivered messages to all the London branches asking them to get all their members there. One of the leaders, Graham Marsden, boss of the south-west London group, said he thought he could get at least fifty.

"Everyone's pissed off round here. I get about three enquiries a day from people wanting to join. I've had to turn away a few; some are real nutters, the sort who'd give us a bad name. We want ordinary white folk to join, more and more, so that eventually there'll be a tidal wave of us and we'll be able to wipe those immigrants out, like a massive tsunami," he said, sweeping out his arms as if flattening a huge area.

I was given the job of collecting leaflets from the printers. They showed the successes we'd had, like stopping a local pub being turned into a community centre for migrants and helping reinstate a council worker who'd been sacked because someone said she was a racist. I was taking a short cut through the next estate when my phone rang. I stopped and looked for the phone in my bag, pulling out several leaflets at the same time. I was shoving them back in when I heard voices behind me, talking Jamaican. I turned and saw three black men coming towards me. A leaflet fluttered to the ground in front of them. I scrambled to get it but one of them got there first. He picked it up.

"Littering the street," he said, sucking his teeth. "We can't have that."

He was looking at the Union Jack and flicked it with his finger.

"Ah, that beautiful symbol of unity; well done, I expect you're spreading the gospel of racial harmony. Let's see."

He opened it and the other two bent to look. They shook their heads and tutted. I started to go but one of them moved round and was blocking my path.

"We don't want your sort round here. We like it nice, no mess around the place, you understand?"

The biggest one who was doing all the talking whispered something in another's ear. My heart was thudding so loud I thought they'd hear. I was as good as dead.

Instead, to my shock, they started laughing. I looked at them, hating them for their confidence and their disdain.

"Give me the rest of those leaflets," the big one said, holding out his hand.

I hesitated and he advanced towards me. I pulled out the whole bundle and gave them to him.

"Now piss off. If we see you round here again you'll be mincemeat."

They moved aside and I turned to run. I could still hear them laughing as I ran round the corner. I didn't stop until I was out of the estate. Fuck. I was meant to be keeping stuff under wraps.

I told Tyler that the printers had made a mistake on the front page and were going to redo them. I was going to have to find the money to pay for the new lot but at least he believed my story.

20

VALERIE

Renee was making me one of her delicious omelettes. Her father was French and had taught her how to cook. They were the lightest, most delicious ones I'd ever tasted. I made a salad and we sat down to eat. We talked about ordinary things, friends, films, music, all the things we liked.

When we'd finished I told her about the photo.

"God, that's weird, maybe they're the murderers, you better go to the police."

I didn't answer straight away.

"You are going to tell them? I mean I know they've been corrupt in the past but things have changed."

"Matthew thinks we should find out who those men are so we're going to look for that girl, the one with the scarf."

"You can't do that, it's really dangerous, Valerie. Let the police do it."

She was looking really worried.

"I'll be careful I promise. I have to do something. It stops me feeling so useless and Matthew's OK. I mean he's a bit all over the place but he really wants to help."

"You trust him more than you trust the police then?"

"I think so. He is in an anti-racist organisation, so he must want things to be different."

"But these people are murderers, if they've done it before they could do it again."

I knew I wasn't going to persuade her that it was a good idea so I changed the subject.

"How's the teaching practice?"

"The children are lovely. They don't seem to notice that I don't really know what I'm doing. Trying to teach maths, I'm hopeless," she laughed her face lighting up.

She seemed happy. I thought about the carrier bags full of books in my flat and the empty time I spent there, knowing that I was never going to act again. I loved Renee but I felt separate from her at that moment. I thought about our first year at college, Renee, Anton and me, how full of excitement we'd been and so determined to be good actors; now for three different reasons none of us was still acting.

* * *

I was at the wine bar with Matthew. We chose a table in the corner, which had a good view of the room. It was strange being out with him, like we were on some kind of date. We talked about what to say to her if we saw the girl. He said he didn't think we should show her the photo in case she overreacted. There were two people serving behind the bar and several waiters but I couldn't see her. A different young woman came over and took our order. I asked for an orange juice and Matthew a beer.

When she came back with the drinks I said, "We're looking for someone that we think works here, she's small with long black hair, do you know her?"

She looked a bit suspicious so I said, "I met her at a party. I've forgotten her name, I must have been a bit drunk."

She smiled at that and said, "You probably mean Shelley. She's on her break at the moment, she'll be out again soon."

We drank our drinks and tried to behave normally. After about ten minutes I saw her coming through a door at the back, heading in our direction. I thought the waitress must have told her we were there but she went straight to the next table to take their order. Matthew nodded at me and when she'd finished I touched her arm.

"Excuse me."

She looked round. "Yes?"

She didn't recognise me straight away. I looked different to when I'd seen her last, my hair was shorter and I had make-up on. She took a step back.

"You're the one from the bus stop."

Matthew said, "We were having a drink and Valerie recognised you."

She looked from me to him and back again as if she didn't believe him.

"We need to find out what happened to Anton," Matthew said.

"I told you I don't know what you're talking about."

He smiled at her. "We're not trying to make trouble, we just want to talk to Jimmy."

"I can't help you. I've got to go, there's people waiting to be served."

"Please, it's really important, a friend has been murdered," he said, keeping his voice low.

She looked around to make sure no one was listening,

but the nearest couple were engrossed in each other. "I know Jimmy, he's not involved in anything like that."

"We're not saying it was him, maybe it was someone he knew."

She wavered for a moment and then sat on the edge of a chair. "You should talk to that Chris Mayhew, Jimmy hangs around with him sometimes. I've tried saying he's a cruel person but he doesn't listen."

It was that name again.

"Can you tell us how to find Chris?" Matthew said.

She got up, looking at him as if he was mad. "No way. He'd kill me. I'm not saying anything else. Now leave me alone."

She moved away and went across the room to pick up an order from the bar.

Matthew leaned across the table. "At least now we know they're definitely mates so it could have been Jimmy in the photo. She didn't say anything about the NER but maybe she doesn't know he's involved. She's obviously scared of Chris."

"What do we do now?"

"I don't know yet but we'll think of something. Let's have another drink anyway."

He told me about the AF, how many were involved and what their aims were. Once or twice I caught Shelley looking at us but she stayed well away.

21

JIMMY

Shelley was at my flat and she was mad.

"That crazy woman came to the wine bar last night asking questions. I want to know what's going on."

"Shit, how did she know you worked there?"

"How should I know? Don't blame me; this is about you not me. There was some posh bloke with her who was pushy, kept going on about his friend being murdered."

She was getting louder by the minute. Luckily Mum and Liam were out.

"What did you do?"

"I was busy, I had to get rid of them so I said if there was any trouble it was to do with Chris, not you."

Now the shit was really hitting the fan.

"You shouldn't have done that."

"Why? It's the truth."

She pushed her hair from her face; her mouth was closed and angry.

"Don't interfere with stuff you don't know about."

Without thinking I raised my hand but stopped myself before I hit her. She backed away and looked at me with disgust.

"If you hit me it's over. You used to be lovely and funny, now you're angry all the time." She pulled the belt of her coat tight. "If you're going to tell me what's happening call me, otherwise we're finished."

I stared at her.

"You don't mean that."

"I really do."

She opened the door and went out without a backward glance.

I threw my phone at the wall and it dropped to the floor with a clunk; I didn't bother to find out if I'd broken it. Sounded like they were onto us. If Chris found out Shelley had dropped him in it he'd do his nut.

That night I couldn't sleep. The eczema on my back was spreading and my skin was itching like mad. I hadn't had it since I was a kid and Dad left. I used to get it all over my hands and arms and all the kids at school used to laugh and avoid me like I had a horrible disease.

* * *

I got back from a hard day's work and saw Liam coming out of my room.

"What are you doing?"

"Looking for that shirt you borrowed. I found this instead."

He was holding a piece of paper. It was an NER leaflet.

"Are you involved with this lot? If you are then you're an idiot."

He started reading. "Mass immigration is destroying our English landscape... Do you believe this shit? What about

Great Granddad? He came over from Ireland. You're part of it." He ripped it into shreds. "This is why I'll never invite Nitin round. You're worse than Wayne."

"Fuck you Liam. Why is Nitin so important, you gay or something?"

He took a swing at me but I caught his arm. He said nothing, just stared at me, hatred in his eyes. I let go and he walked out of the room.

* * *

My life was falling apart. Now Shelley and Liam were both on my case and knew far more than they should. I hated Liam for saying I was like Wayne. No way was I stupid. I had politics, I was doing important business, which was different to just being a thug. I needed to get away from home, put some distance between them and me. So far I'd avoided jail and I wanted it to stay that way. I started looking for rooms and after a few days non-stop searching I found a place in Deptford. It was a crap area but I could afford it, just about. Mum gave me a microwave as a present. Liam wasn't there when I left.

There were four blokes and one girl living in the house. The bath had yellow stains and the showerhead was blocked so water only came out one side. I hated sharing a bathroom with people who didn't clean up after themselves. My room was long and narrow and one wall was bare plaster. At one end there was an electric cooker with two rings and a space for the microwave. I wasn't intending to do much cooking anyway.

It was weird being there. For ages I'd wanted to get a

place of my own – thought about what Shelley had said on her birthday about us living together, imagined a beautiful new flat, maybe overlooking the river with a balcony and at night we stand with our arms round each other looking at the lights in the water. Instead my view was of next door's yard which was full of weeds and rubbish.

On my first night in the house I dreamt about the dead man. His face was black, pitch black, like the inside of a tunnel, then it began to get lighter and after a while he turned into a white person, one who looked just like Liam.

22

VALERIE

The lamp by the park gate flickered three times, went off for a few seconds then came on and stayed on. It was always like that, except the sequence of flickers varied, as if each time was a different message.

I wanted it to mean something – wished it was a message from Anton telling me he was still out there. I missed his funny texts, talking into the night about everything to do with acting, what we loved, what we hated. Most of all I missed being close to him. A part of me regretted that we'd spent the night together because now it wasn't just the loss of a friend – my whole body ached. I remembered how it felt at dawn, the awkwardness from the night before had gone, our physical connection seemed more certain and more real. I knew if I tried I'd be able to recall every detail of that night, every colour and touch, every single word but I couldn't let myself because it would hurt too much. I turned away from the window and pushed the memories out of my mind.

Matthew called and said he had some news so I said to come over.

"Nice place," he said, looking around.

I made him a coffee and we sat at the table by the window.

"There are developments. I've been doing some digging into the organisation. They're setting up a big meeting with a group from Scandinavia. It's on the 24th of March. We haven't pinned down the venue yet. I'm going to be there to see who's going in and out."

"I'm coming with you," I said.

"That's not a good idea."

"I have to."

"Look Valerie, it could get nasty."

"How can it be any nastier than it is already? And what have I got to lose anyway?"

He looked sympathetic. "Alright, I see what you mean. If you're sure."

"I'm sure."

"We need to try to get in. The more we find out the better. If Jimmy and Chris are there it'll prove they're definitely in the middle of this thing."

He drained his coffee and stood up.

"I've got to go now. I'll let you know where it's happening as soon as I can. We'll try and get to the truth, it's the least we can do for Anton."

For once he looked me straight in the eye.

* * *

March 24th came quickly. I got ready, putting on jeans, a black coat and a grey hat that covered my hair. I looked in the mirror. I could probably pass for a man but nothing was going to disguise the fact that I was black. I was scared but I was determined.

The meeting was at a place just south of Tower Bridge. We met at the Tube and started walking. Apart from when he asked if I was OK neither of us said anything. We turned into the narrow street and slowed our pace. Up ahead a man stopped outside one of the buildings and rang the bell. We walked past, pretending to be deep in conversation. Inside a bouncer was checking someone's ID. At the end of the street we turned the corner.

"I was hoping there'd be a pub or cafe nearby so we could watch people, but there's nothing," Matthew said.

"There's no way we can get in. That guy's massive and they must have a list of all the people attending," I said, adrenalin starting to run through my body. I pulled my hat further down over my hair.

"Maybe there's another entrance. Let's look."

We walked back and then noticed a narrow alleyway close to the main door. We ducked in. There was a side door further down, which must be the fire exit. As we stood there, trying to decide what to do, a black man in a chef's uniform came out. He lit a cigarette. Matthew put his arm round me and for a moment I thought he was going to try to kiss me but he whispered, "He looks alright, let's ask him about the meeting."

"OK."

We went over to him.

"Did you know there's a group of racists meeting in this building?" Matthew asked.

The man took a puff on his fag – he looked hot and tired.

"Is that right? Yeah, actually I believe it. They've had stuff like that here before. They say it's legit but you should hear the punters in the bar afterwards. They come out with some evil shit."

"Can you let us in? We're trying to find out what they're doing."

He looked from Matthew to me then shook his head. "Sorry. If they find out it was me I'll get the sack."

"Someone in there might have killed my boyfriend," I said.

His eyes widened. He rubbed the fag out on the wall. "In that case…" He pushed open the door and gestured for us to go inside. He led us through a large kitchen and pointed to the stairs at the end of the corridor. "Up there, turn right and down the end, it's the last room on the left. Be careful."

We got to the next landing and crept along the carpeted corridor until we came to the last door. It was large with a brass doorknob.

Matthew whispered, "When I open it we go straight in. Keep a look out for the two in the picture. I'll try to get a photo."

By then my heart was pounding and my mouth was dry. The reality of what we were about to do was sinking in. I wanted to turn and run down the corridor.

Matthew put his hand on my shoulder and mouthed, "We'll be fine," then he turned the knob. We crept in.

Light was coming from a screen at the front. The room was packed with people watching a film. We stood with our backs against the wall. No one seemed to notice our presence.

Images of black people, faces of suicide bombers, pictures of blood on the ground, a black man holding a knife, all these flickered across the screen. The voice-over was listing how many white people had been killed and how many more were going to die. In between was loud music with crashing cymbals. My stomach was starting to churn with fear. The sides of the room were dark but as my eyes got accustomed to it I could make out flags with the cross of St George. On one wall, to my shock, was a swastika.

Someone shouted, "Who the fuck are you?" A second later the lights flashed on, heads turned to look. A sea of white faces staring. I shrank against the wall as if trying to push myself through it. For a moment nobody moved then someone made a grab for Matthew. A voice at the front yelled, "Get them out."

Matthew was shouting, "Fascists. We know who you are, murderers. You can't hide from us."

I was scanning faces and saw a man with short brown hair who could be the one in the photo. He turned and noticed me and we stared at each other. A man grabbed my arm and started dragging me backwards.

"Get your hands off," I shouted but he tightened his grip.

"This is a dangerous place for you, black bitch," he hissed in my ear.

Two men were pushing Matthew out of the door. In the corridor they shoved him up against a wall and began thumping him. I screamed at them to stop, trying to get away from the one holding me but he put both arms round my waist and I could feel his hot breath in my neck. My mind filled with terror. Then a second later I kicked him hard on the shin. He swore and let go. One of the other men was about to throw a punch at Matthew so I grabbed his arm. Matthew shoved the other, took hold of my hand and we ran, back down the stairs and through the kitchen. The chef wasn't there so we pulled open the back door, raced down the road and dodged into an alleyway opposite. We were both panting like crazy, Matthew was holding his stomach and groaning.

"Shit, the bastards, are you OK?"

"I think so. Are you?"

He felt his ribs. "Yeah, don't think anything's broken. Thanks for wading in."

My arm was throbbing. I leant against the wall trying to stop my legs shaking.

"I'm really sorry I got you into that," he said.

I was crying but I was furious too.

"That stuff they were showing. It made me feel sick. Jimmy was there – he looked up when I called his name. I wanted to get a photo but one of them grabbed me," I said.

"I saw Chris, so that means they're both involved. The bloke at the front must be the new leader. I've not seen him before but I'd recognise him again. He was with some bloke who looked Scandinavian." He straightened up and grimaced. "That hurt, the fuckers." Then all of a sudden he laughed.

Like it was some kind of a game.

23

JIMMY

There was noise at the back of the room. Lights flashed on. I turned and saw bouncers wrestling a man.

He was shouting. "I've got pictures of two of you, Chris and Jimmy, the night my mate was killed. Murderers!" He screamed as the bouncer twisted his arm, trying to shut him up.

I stood up trying to see who it was and saw a black woman. She was over my side of the room, scanning faces. For a moment our eyes locked then one of the security guards grabbed her.

Tyler was calling people to order.

"Keep calm, everyone, the situation's under control."

People were sitting down. The film was frozen on the screen, a close-up of a black man's face, twisted in anger. Chris was heading over to my side of the room. I had to play innocent.

"Fucking reds trying to break up the meeting," I said.

"How did they know our names?"

"I dunno, never seen them before. I thought the security in this place was tight."

"It should be. Keep your head down, don't let anyone see you're bothered."

"We'll start the film again in a minute when we've secured the building," Tyler called out. Then he beckoned us over. He didn't look pleased.

"Who the hell were they?"

"I don't know, sorry," I said. Chris shook his head.

"We can't have anything jeopardising the project. Get after them, make sure it never happens again."

"We will. I promise you won't hear any more about it," Chris said.

"That better be the truth," Tyler said.

"Right, let's get after them, find out who they are," Chris said, pulling on his jacket.

I wanted to delay things. If it was the same people who were harassing Shelley it would all come out about the scarf.

"I'm desperate for a piss."

"For fuck's sake, Jimmy. Get on with it then."

By the time we got outside the two of them had disappeared.

"Someone must have tipped them off about the meeting. Have you been talking to that girlfriend of yours?"

I had to deflect attention away from Shelley so I said the first thing that came in my head.

"I think Liam might know something."

Chris was looking at me with a weird expression. I should have kept my mouth shut but now I'd said it I'd have to make up some story.

"I haven't said anything but he's clever... Maybe he overheard me on the phone to you."

"We haven't talked on the phone. You must have been shooting your mouth off."

"I told you I've kept quiet."

24

VALERIE

We were still in the alleyway when we heard voices. I looked out. Chris and Jimmy were twenty metres away, heads close together, talking. All the anger that I'd been holding down welled to the surface. Without saying a word I turned out of the alley and began walking towards them.

"What are you doing?" Matthew called after me, panicking. I didn't answer. I was getting close. They turned and saw me and for the first time I got a good look at them. Their faces bleached by the streetlamps – Chris's round and bloated, Jimmy's thin and young-looking.

They looked at me as if they couldn't believe I was there. I stopped when I was a few yards away.

"Who murdered my boyfriend?"

There was a moment's silence. Time seemed to stand still. I felt as if I was watching myself on a film. An expression of fear crossed Jimmy's face like a shudder then Chris laughed. Loud and false.

"Ha, ha, we've got a comedian that breaks into buildings. You stupid or what, you think we're telling you anything?"

Jimmy opened his mouth, like a fish looking for air. "You're talking shite. We don't know anything about no murder." He was leaning against the wall in an attempt to be casual. His eyes were very dark. He looked fragile. Behind him the water from a drainpipe was dripping down the bricks making a line of green algae. At that moment I knew he was covering up for Chris.

Matthew caught hold of my arm. "Valerie, let's go." I pulled away.

I said, looking only at Jimmy, "I think you should tell me what happened."

Chris was coming towards me, arms at his sides, flexing his fists. "And I think you should fuck off before you end up like your boyfriend."

Matthew got hold of my arm again and this time I didn't shake him off.

"It's alright, we're going," I said.

Jimmy pulled himself away from the wall and stood close to Chris.

"Yeah, fuck off. We'll let you go this time, but next…"

I took one more look at them, imprinting their faces on my memory and then turned and walked away, Matthew beside me. We walked in silence for a minute.

He turned back once. "They're not following. That was mad. And brave."

"It was them who did it. Chris practically admitted it and Jimmy's scared."

Underneath the vicious swaggering I'd seen the soft belly of fear.

25

JIMMY

Chris reckoned we'd scared them off but I knew he was wrong. The woman was crazy. She looked at me as if she could see right inside. I kept my door double-locked when I was at home and didn't answer my phone unless I was sure who it was.

I promised Chris I'd warn Liam off because otherwise he was going to do it himself but me and him still weren't speaking and if I said anything it was going to make it worse so I did nothing. Everything was fucked up, plus, since Shelley had gone off I was single again.

That night I called Danny and we went to a club. A girl on the dance floor was giving me the eye. She was pretty; long blonde hair, sexy-looking. I went over and did some moves in front of her, she giggled and said something to her mates, then started dancing up against me.

"My name's Marie," she said, into my ear. The way she said it gave me a hard-on.

I was drinking straight vodka instead of my usual lager. Me and Marie were chatting and messing around on the dance floor for a few hours then she asked me back to hers. I said yes. Before we'd even got to the taxi place we were against a wall and she was kissing me. Suddenly Shelley's face flashed before me and I pulled away.

"What's the matter?" she said.

"I'm not in the mood, sorry, nothing to do with you, maybe another time."

She looked angry. "Do you think I'm going to sit around waiting until you decide you want me? Grow up." Then she turned and marched off towards the taxi rank. I thought about calling after her but didn't. I must have been more cut up about Shelley than I thought. She got in a cab; when it passed she'd already turned her face away.

Next day I had a banging head. I'd forgotten that always happened when I drank spirits. I just got to the bathroom before I threw up. Back in my room I lay down and went straight back to sleep. Sometime later I was woken by my mobile ringing somewhere in the room and remembered I was meant to be starting a new job with Ray. I let it ring and stayed in bed, sleeping off and on, like I'd been drugged.

26

VALERIE

Matthew called round next day. "I tried to phone a couple of times but you didn't pick up. I'm sorry you got mixed up in that, it was too dangerous," he said, sounding worried which sort of surprised me.

"It's alright, we survived, didn't we?" I gave a half laugh.

"You're a strong person, Valerie."

He didn't know how I'd lain awake after the confrontation, my body rigid with terror, seeing their faces over and over again, each time more ugly and more malevolent. He didn't know about my decision to give up acting. He didn't know I felt like nothing.

"Did you go to the doctor?"

He shook his head. "They're just bruises. I didn't want them asking questions about how I got them, same with the cops. We kind of broke into the building."

He sat on the sofa, in the same position that Anton had been the last night he was there. I was thinking about how beautiful he'd looked then and how happy I'd been.

Matthew interrupted my thoughts, "Would you like to go out for a drink with me sometime? Not to that same wine bar though," he said and laughed.

I came back to the present, trying to take in his words.

He looked hopeful, pleased with himself.

"Are you asking me out?" Anger was welling up inside. "After all that's happened, do you think I'd go out with you, with anyone," I could hear my voice getting louder, "so soon after Anton's been murdered? I thought you were trying to find out who killed him and all along it's because you fancied me."

His face was really pale, like he was frozen.

"It's not like that Valerie. I've got to really like you, that's all. I do know how much he meant to you."

I wanted to cry and scream across the huge gulf that was between us. He'd never understand what it was like to have ancestors who'd been kidnapped, chained, sold, tortured, murdered. He'd never know the feelings that run deep into history, bodies and minds continuing to remember the trauma. I didn't know him well enough to try to explain and now I never would know him any better.

"If you understood anything you wouldn't have asked."

"Sorry if I upset you. I better go."

He got up and went to the door. He opened it then felt in his pocket and brought out a piece of paper.

"I forgot this. Jake found out where Jimmy lives, don't ask me how. Do you want it?"

I stretched out my hand and took it to make him go away though I didn't know what I'd do with it.

After he'd gone I lay on the floor and stared at the ceiling. I wanted to disappear completely, to retreat back to where I'd come from, back to the tiny seed I'd been. From there I could choose not to be born. I didn't want to kill myself but at that moment I didn't want to be in the world.

* * *

I couldn't tell Renee about the confrontation with Jimmy and Chris, or about Matthew. It would just confirm everything that she feared. I felt lost. Nothing seemed to make sense. I wouldn't miss Matthew but him going meant I was face to face with the bleakness of my life.

I pulled on my coat and hat and went out with no clear idea where I was heading. I got on the first bus that came along, a number 53. It went past where Mr Thomas lived. I knew I wanted to see him. I should have phoned first but hoped he wouldn't mind if I just turned up.

When he answered the door he looked surprised then pleased.

"Hello Valerie, come in, nice to see you."

We went into the kitchen, which seemed a more intimate place than the living room. The walls were painted a sort of pinky-orange. The boiler hummed loudly. The window looked over the next garden. Someone had hung their washing out, a white shirt, the arms waving in the wind.

"I'll make some tea," he said, and put the kettle on.

We sat opposite each other at the small table.

"How are you?" I said.

There was a pause then gradually he started to talk.

"I just exist. I think of him every day. Sometimes I speak to him, about ordinary things, but still…" He paused and I nodded, wanting him to continue. "I didn't realise how much space he took up, the world seems shrivelled without him."

It was as if he too had shrunk, his cheeks were hollow; he looked less like Anton than before. The boiler stopped humming for a moment and there was silence then he said, "And how are you?"

It was OK talking to him. He would understand.

"Nothing seems to make sense and the world looks ugly. As if no one cares about anyone else."

"It's hard, coming to terms with such a terrible thing, how can the world make sense after that? Perhaps you have more grieving to do."

He looked so sympathetic that I started to cry. He didn't try to stop me.

"Was it like this when your wife died?" I said, when I could speak again.

"I missed her deeply of course but Anton was so young and there was no warning. Plus there is someone to blame, not just death."

"Do you think it'll be easier when the person is caught?"

His expression changed. "Maybe but I am not interested in revenge. I don't agree when people say we should bring back the death penalty. It's not the answer. What I want is for the guilty person to see that, not only have they taken away my boy's life but also they've hurt many people. They have also scarred themselves; if they could acknowledge that…"

After he'd spoken we sat in silence for a while. We drank more tea and I noticed how close I felt to him.

"Tell me how the acting is going," he said. "I remember Anton saying that you loved Shakespeare. My favourite is *King Lear*."

I didn't want him to be disappointed in me so I didn't

tell him I'd given it up, instead I said I was waiting for the right role to come along.

When I left he said, "The world is still yours, remember that."

I thought about revenge. If Jimmy and Chris were the murderers did I want them dead? Even though I would hate them, I knew the answer was no. What I wanted was justice and that was different. I had to make them realise what was lost.

* * *

The piece of paper with Jimmy's address was on the mantelpiece in front of the small mirror. Flat 1, 27 Lightwood Road, Deptford. I could tear it into small pieces and put it in the bin. I could get on with my life and let the police do their job.

I put on the red coat that I'd bought at the beginning of the winter and still hadn't worn. It was the red of poinsettia flowers, long and fitted, with a big collar. I slipped the address in the pocket, picked up my umbrella and went out. I took the bus to Deptford. If someone knew what I was doing they would think I was crazy.

Lightwood Road was in the south of the borough. I found number 27, a run-down three-storey house. It had a lot of bells. Flat 1 must be downstairs. I walked past slowly then turned and went past again. The window had greyish coloured nets with a tear down one side. The curtains were half drawn and there was a light on. I thought about ringing the bell then decided it was a bad idea. Instead I went and stood on the other side of the road. I had a sense of being outside myself. It started to rain hard so I put up the umbrella.

27

JIMMY

In the evening I dragged myself out of bed my stomach cramped with hunger. I pulled the curtains open and looked out. It was dark and pissing down. Someone was standing under the lamp post on the other side of the road. Colour glowing under the light – a black woman in a red coat, still as a statue. Something about the way she was standing was familiar.

I drew back behind the curtain watching her. A van passed by at speed, sending out a wave of water that must have soaked her but she still didn't move. I wanted to get rid of her but then she'd know for sure it was the right address so I watched TV and waited. After ten minutes I looked again but she was still there. It was like being under siege. I sat down again, trying to ignore her presence. The next time I looked she'd gone and I wondered if I'd imagined it all. Maybe I was really sick.

I went to the King's Head looking for Chris. I needed to know if she was after him as well. The pub was crowded, men talking at the bar, groups of young women crowded round tables, hair polished, showing flesh. Normally I'd want to chat one up but I had other things on my mind.

I found Chris with a group of his mates and told him we needed to talk.

Outside he said, "What's up?"

"That woman's stalking me."

He laughed into his pint, which sprayed over my jacket. "You should be so lucky, look at the state you're in, you couldn't pull anyone."

"I'm serious. It's that black woman from the meeting. She knows where I live."

"You're getting paranoid."

"I swear it's her. She's watching my house. Have you seen her round yours?"

"Nah mate – sounds like you're imagining things. Get a grip – you're falling apart. Remember what's at stake. It's your neck as well as mine." He did a chopping motion with his hand across his throat. "Deal with it."

He turned and started walking back to the door. I couldn't believe he was just leaving me with the problem. I grabbed his arm and pulled him round, forgetting our difference in size.

"This is your mess Chris, you need to clean it up."

He looked surprised that I was standing up to him and for a moment I felt triumphant but then he lifted his fist and I saw it coming for my face; I tried to duck but he caught me on the side of the head and I spun round and hit the ground hard.

I heard him say, "Not a chance in hell, Jimmy." The pub door slammed.

I lay on the ground, head throbbing, face in a puddle. I couldn't go any lower. We were real enemies now. If things got bad he might even try to pin the murder on me. I still had the NER, without that I was fucked.

I was paranoid at home, thinking the woman was going to be there again. I bought cans of lager. It helped me get to sleep but I woke up in the early hours with a dry mouth, head throbbing, my heart thudding in my chest. At work I was more and more knackered. One day I put grey gloss on a wall when it should have been emulsion. Ray went mad, making me stay back to sort it out.

"What's going on, Jimmy? You look like death. I thought you wanted to get somewhere in this trade?"

I said the first thing that came into my head. "Me and Shelley are going through a bad patch. She keeps going on about wanting to get married and settle down, I'm not ready, it's driving me mad."

For once he didn't sound sympathetic. "Sort things out, I can't have your personal life affecting my business."

* * *

She was there again, this time standing at the bottom of the steps, looking as if she was going to come up and ring the bell. I had to stop her from talking to the others in the house. I pulled on my jacket and looked for my keys, which weren't in the pocket. By the time I got outside she'd gone. I looked both ways and thought I saw her up near the shops. Trying to keep my eyes on her I followed at a fast walk. There were still quite a few people around. Outside the bookies an old man grabbed hold of my arm, breathing alcohol fumes all over me. I shoved him off me and looked to see where she was but there was no sign of her.

I was outside the old cinema. Dead buddleia flowers were growing through the cracks; the domed roof looked like it was caving in. The window at the top was broken, a blue curtain hung through, wet and dirty. The 'For Sale' sign had been there forever.

There was an entrance at the side with an overflowing bin and a metal door. It had been forced open. Maybe she'd gone in, she was weird enough to do anything. I pushed the door.

It was pitch dark at first then my eyes started to make out rows of abandoned seats. Some were broken and the material stained with damp. At the back was a stage. The curtains that hung at the sides were torn and limp. Blue paint was peeling from the walls and ceiling and a chandelier was hanging down at a precarious angle. It stank of urine.

I shouted, "You don't scare me."

There was silence. All I could hear was dripping then a high-pitched laugh sounded from somewhere above. I looked up but there was no one on the balcony.

"Leave me alone," I yelled, louder.

The voice called, "Alone, alone, alone, you're alone," like an echo, followed by another screaming laugh. I got out as fast as I could.

* * *

I was lying on the pavement – a full moon overhead. The woman was there, looking down at me. She began to speak. At first I thought she was speaking another language then I began to make out the words.

"Your mind's been stolen. You need to catch the thief. It's not too late."

From behind her a man appeared. He took her arm and

led her away. The ground was cold and hard. I woke up and the duvet was on the floor; my body limp as if all the juice had drained out of me.

When I got to work two hours late Ray opened the door and stood blocking the hallway. Behind him was a young man stripping wallpaper.

"Sorry Jimmy. I've given you enough warnings. I need someone reliable."

He handed me an envelope. "Here's this week's wages. You're going to have to learn to get out of bed on time if you want to keep a job."

I could tell by his expression there was no point arguing so I took the money and didn't say a word, just walked away. I went to a cafe and ordered beans and chips. While I was waiting I opened the envelope. There was an extra £20 on top of my wages but my rent was due, which would leave me £90 to last until I could get another job.

When I opened the door to my room it smelt disgusting. I'd had fish and chips one night and left some. The bin didn't have a lid on it. I sat on the bed drinking lager, trying to figure out how I'd got in such a mess. Things went round in my head. I thought about calling Shelley and saying, 'Let's start again, go to Spain or Portugal, get a job in a cafe by the beach, forget about everything that's happened.'

I hurled the can across the room. It hit the wall, spraying lager all over the place. The bare plaster turned dark pink, like the inside of flesh. Nothing was going to work because the main problem, the one I couldn't fix, was that I was involved in a murder.

For weeks I'd been blaming Chris for everything. He'd

killed someone and ruined my life but for a few seconds I'd hesitated: If I'd stayed to see if he was alive, phoned for an ambulance, waited until it came; if I'd done any of those things maybe he'd be OK, maybe I'd be OK.

28

VALERIE

I knew Jimmy had spotted me. I crossed the road and jumped on a bus heading north. As the bus scudded past the park I smiled to myself. The fact that he knew I was onto him gave me a sense of power.

Close to a bus stop was a large hoarding. While we waited for people to get on I gazed at a poster for the new production of *Macbeth*. The face of the lead actor stared back with a haunted expression.

Back at the flat I picked up the bag of books that I'd left by the door, meaning to take to a charity shop, and emptied it out. I took up my copy of *Macbeth*, seeing how neatly it fitted into my hands. Pulling a chair close to the radiator I began reading, listening to the rhythm of the words, which sounded both familiar and exciting. I was gripped by Macbeth's speech to Banquo's ghost, the images perfectly conjuring the terror in his mind. I read and read, soaking up the story, like a drug that I'd given up and then succumbed to.

When I got to the end I remembered Jimmy's face at the window and how vulnerable he looked. Was he starting to feel guilty? Was his conscience beginning to torture him?

Perhaps the tide was turning.

In my possession were a lot of pieces of information that, individually, weren't much help but could add up to something substantial. I needed to try and use them.

Leonard, who I'd met at Matthew's, was writing about far right groups and might be willing to help but the only way I could get in touch with him was through Matthew and we hadn't spoken since the night he'd asked me out. I couldn't let my feelings get in the way though so I sent a brief but friendly text asking for Leonard's email. I didn't explain why I wanted it but he'd work it out. He texted back straight away with the address, ending with 'hope u r ok.'

In my email to Leonard I said something about the situation and that I needed some advice. He suggested a cafe in town where we could talk. When we met I was embarrassed at first and wondered whether I should trust him but he was friendly and I started to relax. He had a sorrowful looking face, with large bags under blue eyes, which made me wonder about his life.

"I'm so sorry about Anton, your boyfriend, it is tragic and appalling."

I told him more about that night and what it had been like for me. He was a good listener and I said more than I'd meant to. I told him about the scarf, meeting Matthew and breaking into the NER meeting. I also said that I knew where Jimmy lived, but not that I'd been there because I didn't want him to think I was crazy. He said he knew quite a lot about the NER and that they were capable of organising and covering up a murder.

"The scarf sounds like a connection, though I agree that the police might think it's fanciful. I do think they'd be interested in the email and the photograph." He took a sip from his coffee. "I'll consult a friend who's a lawyer. She's one of the best there is and will know how to proceed. The police will be following leads of their own but perhaps this extra knowledge will make a difference to getting a conviction. I promise to do everything I can to assist. I know how painful it is to not have justice."

For the first time in weeks I felt as if someone was really on my side.

"Thank you," I said. "I'm really glad I asked you."

He smiled, his face lifted and he looked quite different.

I asked him why he did the work he did.

"My grandfather sent my mother to England from Germany in 1938 when she was seventeen. They were working-class Jews and he didn't have the money to take the whole family so he and my grandmother and youngest son stayed behind. They died in a concentration camp."

Although a part of me already knew what he was going to say I was still shocked. I'd lost Anton but not my whole family. Here was someone who understood about trauma, about loss, about being killed for who you were. He wasn't just fighting because his head told him to but because his heart drove him to it.

"I'm so sorry."

"I write about it because I want to make sure things don't happen again on that scale but the current situation is also frightening. Again the government are blaming people, this time immigrants and the poor for the economic problems that they themselves have created." He stopped and smiled.

"I'm lecturing. Of course you already know this. Tell me some other things about yourself. I remember Matthew saying you were an actor."

"Yes, I am," I said, forgetting I'd given it up. "I really love Shakespeare, that's where I started, although I'm interested in contemporary theatre as well." I told him about *Wounded Home* and he said he'd heard it was very good.

"Next time you perform I would love to come."

When we left the cafe he said, "I'll get in touch with Rosalind straight away and give you a call as soon as I hear back."

29

JIMMY

Light was coming through the tear in the net curtain. I didn't know what time it was and I didn't care. There was no point getting up. There'd be nothing at the Job Centre. I couldn't get a job in a shop or a cafe because I was useless with money. Numbers always got jumbled up in my head. The doorbell rang and I heard voices in the hall. I thought they must be for someone else then there was a knock on my door. I didn't answer.

Shelley's voice called through the keyhole, "Jimmy, it's me, are you there?"

I sat up. There were shapes of clothes everywhere. She called again.

"Hang on."

I pulled on jeans and a T-shirt. I could smell my sweat but there was nothing I could do about it. She came in, sniffed and wrinkled her nose. She stepped over the clothes, went to the window and drew the curtains.

She was wearing a new purple coat and her hair was tied back. I'd forgotten how beautiful she was.

"Sorry about the room, I've been really busy."

"I don't care about that, I want to talk to you about something."

"What?" I said, licking my lips, which were dry as a bone.

She turned to the side, her profile against the window, looking far away and grown up.

"I'm pregnant."

It was the last thing I expected to hear. I thought maybe she'd figured out about the murder but not that. I starèd at her and she looked back, holding my gaze, she wasn't smiling.

"You're what?"

She repeated the words.

"You can't be, we always used condoms." Then I remembered that one had come off and we'd laughed about it.

My mind was going nuts trying to take it in. I couldn't imagine her pregnant. She was so slim and so young.

"I found out two weeks ago. I wasn't going to tell you but then I changed my mind."

It seemed like weeks since we'd had sex. I tried to figure out the timing of it but couldn't even remember what day it was.

"How do you know it's mine?" I wanted to hurt her. I wanted to see her cry – that would be better than her coldness.

She held her handbag across her stomach as if protecting herself.

"You're cruel Jimmy. First you threaten me, now you accuse me of going off with someone else. You used to love me."

I still loved her but I couldn't have her, not after everything that'd happened.

"Whatever you think I know that you're the father and I came to tell you I'm keeping it. If you want to be involved I need proof you've changed. I don't want any more violence with a baby around."

"I've got no money," I said.

"It's not money I want, Mum and Dad will help out. I can live at home until after the baby's born."

"When…?"

"It's due in September."

I didn't know what else to say. My life was fucked up and this was the worst timing.

"Well, anyway, I'm going now. You've got my number."

She went out of the door.

I put my arms around my knees and rocked on the bed, imagining the baby. I'd never thought about having children. It was something that happened to other people; older, boring people. All those nappies and crying. I wondered if it was a boy or a girl, if she knew. Shelley was the sort of person who wouldn't want to find out until it was born. It would have my blue eyes and her black hair. Then I thought about my dad and how he wasn't there after I was eleven. I wouldn't want that to happen to my baby. My eyes were burning as if the tears behind couldn't be squeezed out. The eczema on my back itched and burned like it would never stop.

30

VALERIE

I was on my way to Leonard's place for a meeting. The lawyer had asked for everything I knew to be written in chronological order in a printed document, which she would then take to the police.

Arriving at the large four-storey house in West Dulwich I climbed the steps and rang the bell. Leonard opened the door. "Welcome."

We went into a high-ceilinged room that seemed to be full of things. One wall was entirely covered in a bookshelf and the mantelpiece was crammed with framed photographs. On the large desk were piles of folders.

"Sit down," he said, gesturing to a seat. "I'll just get us some coffee."

He went out and came back with a coffee pot and mugs on a tray. He poured me a mug of the dark, aromatic liquid and then we both sat at his desk.

We went through everything that'd happened since Anton's murder. Some of the order was confused in my head, especially in the days soon after, but gradually I got it straight. Shelley at the bus stop wearing the scarf, her reaction when I first confronted her, meeting Matthew, the photo sent to Jake, then later the NER meeting with Jimmy and Chris.

Leonard noted everything on his computer, which I then checked.

"Because of Rosalind's reputation the police will take her seriously. At this stage you don't need to go but I'm sure they will want to interview you at some point."

I felt a spark of fear, as if it was me who had done something wrong and had to remind myself that it was progress.

He looked at the clock. "I have to go now I'm afraid. I've got another meeting."

We came out of the house and down the steps. It was another freezing night and the streets were deserted. We began to walk in the direction of the Tube, treading carefully through the ice and snow.

31

JIMMY

Shelley's visit shook me up. Whatever happened with her and the baby I needed money fast. The rent was due and I was down to my last packet of fags. None of my mates had any money so I had to get some sort of work.

I went to Tyler's office and said I wanted to earn some quick cash. I'd do anything.

"As it happens I do need someone. If there's a good outcome I'll make sure you're well paid."

He didn't tell me much about the job but I got the idea someone was digging dirt on the organisation and they wanted him stopped. It meant I was getting in even deeper but I didn't have a choice. It was that or begging.

I was given an address in the posh part of Dulwich and told to watch the house in the evenings, see when the man came in and out and if there was a pattern to his movements.

The first night it snowed. There was a shop doorway across the road from the house so I hung out there, smoking fag after fag, trying to keep warm. Not a lot happened. The next night a tall grey-haired man came out of the house at about 7 p.m. He came back an hour later. The next night it was the same and the next. He was always alone and moved slowly. It was hard to believe he was much of a threat. After five nights I reported to Tyler that the pattern was the same. He told me I was to do one more night and this time when the man came out I was to call him straight away. After that I was getting paid.

It was as cold as ever. I walked up and down not caring if I drew attention to myself. It was nearly 8 p.m. when I saw the door open. Close behind him was someone else. When the person came into the light I saw it was her.

She was everywhere – in my dreams, outside my house, now here. For a moment I forgot the phone call. I watched as they came down the steps, then I remembered and dialled the number, letting it ring three times. They passed me on the opposite side of the road then began to cross over. At that moment a car flew round the corner. Instead of swerving or sounding the horn the driver headed straight at them.

Without thinking I shouted, "Look out!"

The woman screamed and grabbed the man's arm. I waited for the sound of a thump but the car missed them by inches. It almost hit a parked vehicle then swerved back to the other side of the road and with a screech of tyres sped off. I caught the last two letters of the number plate – BZ – Billy's car.

They were both on the ground. For a moment nothing happened then she got up and started helping him to his feet. She looked around as if frightened the car might come back. I ducked my head down and started to walk away, trying to stay upright on the freezing snow.

32

VALERIE

There was a shout. A car, headlights blazing, was heading straight for us; the shiny metal bumper level with my hips. I grabbed Leonard, he knocked into me and we both fell backwards. I heard a groan as the breath was knocked out of him. I lay still for a second, snow cold against my cheek, convinced that the car was going to come back a second time then I got up, my heart beating fast. I looked around to see where the voice had come from. Across the road a figure in a dark jacket was walking away. I could have sworn it was Jimmy.

Leonard was sitting up and I put a hand under his arm to help him up.

"Are you hurt?" I asked.

He was brushing snow off his trousers. "Nothing broken, are you alright?"

"OK I think. That was scary."

"The car must have skidded on the ice," he said.

It seemed obvious that it was deliberate though I didn't know if it was aimed at me, or him. How would anyone have known I was going to be there? I'd only been to the house once before.

I got my mobile out. "I'll call the police."

"No, no." He put his hand on my arm. "Don't waste their time." He looked up and down the street, which was now empty. "There are no witnesses and you didn't get a number plate, did you?"

I shook my head. "I wasn't quick enough."

"The main thing is that you're OK." He smiled his sorrowful smile. "Shall we carry on?"

I had the feeling that he knew the car was aimed for him. I hesitated then said, "I think I'll go the other way. There's someone in Deptford I'd like to see."

"Of course. We'll be in touch soon. Take care."

As soon as he'd gone I turned and walked back the way Jimmy had gone. The snow was falling hard, flakes drifting into my face, some onto my lips. Once or twice I skidded but managed not to fall. Jimmy was probably way ahead of me by now. The streets were quiet, as they always were when it snowed, sounds muffled so that London almost lost its identity. I wasn't sure where I was but didn't want to waste time by stopping to look at a map.

After a while I came to a main road which had shops on both sides. I stopped and looked around. There were a couple of people at a bus stop and several in a kebab shop but no one who looked like Jimmy. I hesitated, shivering, while I tried to decide what to do.

A bus went past going to London Bridge so I started walking in that direction. I passed the last of the shops and came to a grassy area in front of a tower block. Ahead of me, slumped on a low wall, was a figure huddled into a jacket, smoking a cigarette.

A force propelled me forward until I was standing in front of him, just out of his reach.

"You," he said, looking at me briefly. His skin was covered in red, scaly blotches.

"Was it you who shouted?"

He took a long drag of the cigarette and shrugged which I took to mean yes.

"They want him, not you."

"Who does?"

"I can't tell you that. He's investigating people, he needs to stop."

"He won't." I couldn't believe I was only a few feet away from a man responsible for Anton's death. On his own he seemed powerless. "If you care about what happens to us then tell me what happened that night. The night Anton was murdered."

I stepped back as I said it, half expecting him to leap up and grab me.

He took a drag on his cigarette then dropped it in the snow. It fizzled out.

"All I can say is it wasn't me."

From the way he said it I knew he meant it was Chris.

"You don't know what it's like when someone you love is murdered; the pain of it. If you did you'd do something about it." I was shaking and my bottom lip was trembling but I wasn't going to cry.

He looked up and for a moment straight at me and I saw a flicker of recognition in his eyes. Then he got up.

"You better warn your friend," he said, and walked away.

* * *

As I watched the dark figure recede the shock of the near accident and being so near to Jimmy began to sink in. I knew I couldn't be on my own that night. Even though it was getting late I made my way to Renee's.

"What's up? Come in, you look freezing."

She made me a cup of tea and I sat on the sofa, surrounded by colourful cushions. I told her about the car that nearly hit us although I said it was just me because she didn't know about Leonard yet and I couldn't tell her I'd talked to Jimmy.

She put her arm round me. "That's awful, God I'm so glad you're OK."

The after-effects were starting to hit me and I felt exhausted. I leant against her and could feel my eyes closing.

"Can I stay here tonight? I can't face going home."

"Of course. We could hang out together tomorrow."

That night I slept better than I'd done for ages. There was a tingling feeling in my body when I woke, as if it had been numb and was slowly coming back to life. I stretched, feeling strength running though my muscles. I remembered the physicality of *Wounded Home* and could sense a desire for that life returning. To have my whole being absorbed in a piece of creativity. Nothing else gave me such a sense of myself.

I was starting to see that giving up on my dreams wasn't going to get justice for Anton.

33

JIMMY

When I looked in the mirror I didn't recognise myself. Eczema had spread to my face and my lips were dry and cracked. My mind was jumping all over the place. The woman's face appeared as if she was standing behind me. She was watching, her eyes following me around the room, she wasn't ever going to go away. I knew I had to talk to someone. There was only one person who might listen.

Liam answered straight away. "What do you want?"

"Can you meet me at the pub?"

"Why?"

"Just being friendly. I'm buying," I said, trying to keep the tremor out of my voice.

"I've got college work."

"Just one drink."

There was silence then he said, "Half an hour at the most."

He arrived after me. I hadn't seen him for a few weeks and he looked different; taller, more handsome, grown up.

"What's up with you Jimmy? You look a right mess, by the way."

"I need to talk."

Words... *I was there when a murder happened...* churned around in my head but none came out of my mouth. I gulped from my pint. Liam had hardly touched his.

"This is a waste of time. If you don't tell me what we're here for I'm going."

I thought about the last time we went fishing, it was only a few weeks ago but it felt like another world. He was getting up.

I said into my drink, "I saw a man get killed."

"What did you say?"

"A man was murdered. Right in front of me."

"How?"

"He was stabbed. Chris did it." As soon as I said it I regretted it and hoped by some miracle he hadn't heard but he was leaning forward, looking at me in horror.

"Are you saying Chris murdered someone?"

I looked around, frightened someone might hear but no one seemed to have noticed anything.

"I didn't say that."

"Yes you did and you need to go to the police."

"He'd kill me."

"You're a fucking coward, Jimmy. You're involved in racist shit and now murder. You're my big brother. I used to look up to you. What happened?" He got up and threw some coins on the table. "I don't want your beer money and I don't want to see you again."

He walked away. I called after him but he didn't turn around.

* * *

I stayed hunched in a corner drinking. Even Liam hated me. The image of the dead man lying on the grass ballooned in my mind. His jacket, his jeans both splattered with mud, blood too if I could have seen it. There was other violence, my violence – the accordion player, the fight in East London. They could easily have turned bad.

Finishing my pint I left the pub and started walking down Cold Blow Lane. It was freezing, wind swirling between the boarded-up warehouses, rattling through the spiked metal on top of the massive gates. I passed a man on his mobile, he was laughing loudly.

At Subway 4, where the fast trains passed over the road, I noticed that someone had cut a hole in the fence. I went to look. A thought occurred. Checking to make sure there was no one about, I forced my way through and started to climb the bank. It was steep – I slipped on a patch of ice and fell forward, scraping my hands on the frozen mud. I needed to get to the top so I grabbed the branch of a small tree and pulled myself up. There were two more fences. The first had no footholds but I pressed my trainers into the chain link, climbed and jumped down into the narrow gap.

A fast train surged past sending a blast of noise and air that hit me like an explosion. The next fence had a wide metal bar on top. I took a deep breath and hauled myself up onto it, holding one of the uprights to stop me falling. The tracks were about six feet in front of me. I could hear another train coming and a second later it hurtled past at 100 miles an hour. It was what I wanted, the noise, the dirt, to be able to disappear along with it. A man was dead, another nearly was, Shelley was pregnant and didn't want me, nor did Liam. The next train was mine.

I heard a shout and turned to see where it came from. A man was standing below me, looking up, the same one that'd been laughing on his phone.

"Are you OK?" He sounded foreign.

"Leave me alone."

"It's not safe, one slip and there'll be no tomorrow."

"I don't want tomorrows."

"Whatever's gone wrong can be sorted out."

"No it can't. Anyway, I like it up here." I did a little skip on the bar, balancing on one leg like a high-wire walker.

"I'm impressed. I've got a son about your age, he goes crazy sometimes too but we talk about things, make it OK."

He sounded like he cared. He'd run a mile if he knew.

"Some things can't be fixed."

When I said it I knew I meant it. It was the only way out because what I'd done couldn't be erased from my mind. I turned away from him.

There was a lull in the trains. I thought the man had gone away. I was pleased – he was probably just trying to make me feel bad or something. Then I heard a noise and realised he'd come up the bank and was climbing the first fence.

"What the fuck are you doing? You're insane."

He had a determined look on his face and was getting somewhere. He got to the top, then he slipped and fell into the gap but he picked himself up straight away and was climbing the last fence. He pulled himself up onto the bar near where I was, panting like crazy. He had to be at least fifty.

"Thought I'd join you. I don't like heights much." He wobbled slightly and grabbed the upright.

"There's no point two of us dying. Get down before the train comes."

I heard it coming. It was my chance but if I jumped he might too, he was that mad.

He shouted, "I'll hold on if you do."

I shut my eyes, I felt myself leaning forwards, pushing towards the void but my fingers were still glued to the metal upright. The noise grew louder – it was now or never. The sound reached its peak and then it was gone, the only thing remaining was the clicking of the rails. I opened my eyes and he was still there.

34

VALERIE

My agent called and left a voicemail message. She had the perfect audition for me, a role I'd always wanted – Viola in *Twelfth Night*. She knew I was taking a month off because of Anton but not that I'd decided to give up acting.

After I'd listened to her message I went out for a walk. I was torn. There was still no justice for Anton but something was calling me back to acting. My perfect role, the one I'd always wanted. I loved the idea of pretending to be a man and all the humour that comes from the deception. I'd seen the all-male *Twelfth Night* at the Globe Theatre with Anton when he'd got back from the States. Mark Rylance was Olivia and from the moment he appeared on stage I was gripped. He wore white make-up and a black dress and his face conveyed sadness, arrogance and trickery. It was difficult to take my eyes off him.

The cold spring had turned; one day, two days, three days. Nature had started to breathe again. The sun was warm on my skin and for a fleeting moment I thought it was possible to be happy again.

That night I lay thinking of Anton. If he'd been alive he might have played my brother in the play. I felt as if I was leaving him behind. Was I being selfish, following my passion? I tossed and turned, wishing I could talk to him. In the morning I knew I had to go to the cemetery.

Anton's ashes had been scattered beside his mother's grave. Cremation was so different to burial, there was nothing left of the person, but still it was a place to go to and perhaps something of his spirit remained. The stone was engraved: 'In Loving Memory to Rose Ada Thomas'. There were three orange lilies in a vase so I knew someone had been in the last few days. As I stood there a man walked past carrying a watering can. He gave me a small smile as if to say, we are two of a kind in this place, joined together in our grieving. I watched as he watered some daffodils on a grave nearby.

It didn't feel right that Anton was in such a quiet place. He hadn't wanted peace, he'd wanted life and everything there was. I kept trying to make sense of it but there was no sense to be made. I spoke to him silently, mouthing the words, telling him of my decision to go for the audition. I said I would never give up fighting for justice but I needed to act. It was who I was. I listened for a response but all I could hear was the sound of small birds in a tree nearby.

* * *

The theatre company were auditioning for three female roles, Olivia, Viola and the maid. The green room was full of women. As often happened, because my surname began with W, I was called last.

Feeling confident and alert I took my position onstage. The director and another man were sitting in the stalls. I gave my name and told them the pieces I was going to perform. The monologues I'd chosen were from *Lady Windermere's Fan* and *Macbeth*. I wanted to prove that I could do both comedy and drama. Immersing myself in the rich words of Oscar Wilde I performed the first of the pieces. When I'd finished I saw that they were both smiling. Pausing I moved to a different place on the stage and began the speech by Lady Macbeth. I loved these words and was looking forward to speaking them.

A slight sound in the wings distracted me. I had to stop myself from turning to see where it came from and for an instant was gripped by panic, thinking I was going to forget the rest of the speech. Remembering how much I wanted the part I took a deep inward breath and carried on but before I reached the end the director said loudly, "Thank you, Ms Wilding, we've heard enough."

I stopped, shocked, and stood looking at him but he nodded and said, "You can leave the stage," then looked down at his notes. There was nothing else to do so I walked off and went back to the green room. Everyone else had gone.

Had I been so bad that they couldn't stand to hear me out? It was as humiliating as when Sarah told me I wasn't pretty enough to play Hermia. Shoving my notes back in my bag I grabbed my jacket and walked through reception to the exit. I was about to open the door when someone called, "Ms Wilding."

I turned and saw the director hurrying after me.

"There you are," he said. "I thought you'd gone. Sorry I interrupted you but we'd heard so many speeches and anyway we knew after your first piece that you were the one."

I made myself look at him. His expression was serious. "Really?"

"Yes, really. You're exactly right for Viola."

I wanted to hug him but he didn't look like the sort of person you hugged so I held out my hand. He took it and said, "We're looking forward to working with you."

35

JIMMY

He waited until I got down before he left. We didn't talk. A bit of me wished I'd thanked him but he didn't seem to want it. I walked all the way home trying to make sense of what'd happened. The man was foreign. I didn't know where from. If he hadn't been there I'd be under that train. He didn't know me and I didn't deserve it but he'd done it anyway.

Billy was round the next night hammering on the door until I let him in. He had a message from Tyler. "No alibi, no payment, from now on you're on your own. You're lucky, if it was down to me I'd have done you over."

For two days I didn't go out. I had thoughts and visions constantly. Now I knew the man's name they were more real and more scary. If I'd stopped and looked in his face, if I'd ignored Chris telling me to run. If…

I tried to push away the terror but it had taken over. I was there with him in the park. I became him. The knife blade was sliding in – there was a twisting agony as Chris pulled it out. Reaching down I put my hand in the hole. My head felt as if it was exploding. I retched and cried out, trying to find words for what I was feeling but they weren't there. I put my hands on the wound, pressing my fingers inwards, pushing and pinching the flesh together, trying to close it. My skin was marked and red. Words still wouldn't come. I pushed harder. Sorry. That was the word I wanted. Sorry, but that wasn't enough, I had to say his name, I'm sorry Anton, first in a whisper then louder. Something burst open inside with a force that shocked. I was crying. I thought I'd forgotten how. I never cried when Wayne was bullying me, it would've made everything worse. Now there was nothing and no one to stop me, I lay on the bed, my whole body shaking. I cried until I was exhausted and then fell asleep. There were no more dreams.

* * *

When I got up the sun was out and the snow was gone. It was proper spring at last. I had a shower, the first one for days, soaped myself all over, neck, back, balls and cock, every nook and cranny. Then I had a shave. After I'd finished I looked in the mirror. The fog in my head had gone and I knew what I had to do.

My suit was hanging in the wardrobe. Next to it was a white shirt that was clean enough. I thought about tidying the room but that could wait. I picked up my keys and headed for the bus stop. I got on a number 37 and sat upstairs, looking out at all the people. They were going to work, doing ordinary things with their lives.

When the bus got to Duke Street I rang the bell and got off. I walked past the Hope and Anchor, the carpet warehouse and the Good Morning Cafe. Stopping in front of a tall building I buttoned my jacket. I climbed the steps. When I got to the top I pushed open the door to the police station.

ACKNOWLEDGEMENTS

A special thanks to Sarah Natalia, who is an inspiration and Jacob, for the wise words and support. Thanks also to Corinne, Jackie, Joan, Jono, Karen, Sandra, Julia and Rob for their encouragement.